BULLET POINTS
VOLUME I

BULLET POINTS
VOLUME I

Nathan W. Toronto
Editor

TORONTO INTERNATIONAL MEDIA

Paperback edition, second impression, July 21, 2022
ISBN 979-8-7536248-1-9

The Arabic block *noon* colophon is a trademark of Toronto International Media.

Cover design by Nathan W. Toronto. Cover © 2022 Nathan W. Toronto. Cover image by Daniil Volkov (used under license).

Other edition: ISBN 978-0-9976550-4-9 (ebook)

To the military officers
I had the privilege to teach
—N. T.

Typset using LATEX.

Preface

WAR IS A TERRIBLE HUMAN ACTIVITY, yet so many of our national rituals—our heroes, our holidays, our venerations—
revolve around the conduct and outcome of war. Most humans recognize the wrongness of doing violence to other humans, yet we also
find justifications for the organized political violence of war. We
accept its tragedy and ignore its complexity, yet tally both its toll
and its glory with equal acceptance. Warfare has certainly changed
over the course of human history, but war as a human institution
appears to march to the beat of its own drum. Forests of trees have
given their lives to unpack these ideas, but if you're curious, Carl von
Clausewitz' *On War*, Book I, is a good place to start to appreciate the
difference between the character and nature of war.

The *Bullet Points* anthology, based on the blog of the same name,
seeks to be "sensitive to the complexity, tragedy, and hope of warfare
and violence in human (and nonhuman) society." During the calendar
year, military fiction stories appear on the blog and remain there
until November, when the anthology goes on sale. Submissions are
open throughout the year, and *Bullet Points* accepts both reprints and
original stories.

The stories in this first *Bullet Points* anthology are organized
chronologically, beginning with an H. G. Wells story from 1903 and
ending with an Eric Fomley story from 2021. The purpose of this is
to show how our thinking about war changes over time. Maybe this
will help us imagine a world without war. Until that happens, we
can enjoy—and reflect upon—*Bullet Points*.

—Nathan W. Toronto, ed.

CONTENTS

The Land Ironclads

H. G. WELLS

> H. G. Wells' "The Land Ironclads" first appeared in *Strand* in 1903, years before the advent of armored warfare in World War I. In fact, the first tank was manufactured in 1915 as a way to break the stalemate of trench warfare. Coincidentally, Ernest Swinton, author of "The Defence of Duffer's Drift," championed this effort from his post in the War Office. H. G. Wells' prescience is yet another example of science fiction authors' uncanny ability to anticipate changes in all areas of life.

THE YOUNG LIEUTENANT lay beside the war correspondent and admired the idyllic calm of the enemy's lines through his field glass.

"So far as I can see," he said, at last, "one man."

"What's he doing?" asked the war correspondent.

"Field glass at us," said the young lieutenant.

"And this is war!"

"No," said the young lieutenant, "it's Bloch."

"The game's a draw."

"No! They've got to win or else they lose. A draw's a win for our side."

They had discussed the political situation fifty times or so, and the war correspondent was weary of it. He stretched out his limbs. "Aaai s'pose it is!" he yawned.

"*Flut!*"

"What was that?"

"Shot at us."

The war correspondent shifted to a slightly lower position. "No one shot at him," he complained.

"I wonder if they think we shall get so bored we shall go home?"

The war correspondent made no reply.

"There's the harvest, of course..."

They had been there a month. Since the first brisk movements after the declaration of war things had gone slower and slower, until it seemed as though the whole machine of events must have run down. To begin with, they had had almost a scampering time; the invader had come across the frontier on the very dawn of the war in half-a-dozen parallel columns behind a cloud of cyclists and cavalry, with a general air of coming straight on the capital, and the defender horsemen had held him up, and peppered him and forced him to open out to outflank, and had then bolted to the next position in the most approved style, for a couple of days, until in the afternoon—*bump!*—they had the invader against their prepared lines of defense. He did not suffer so much as had been hoped and expected. He was coming on, it seemed with his eyes open, his scouts winded the guns, and down he sat at once without the shadow of an attack and began grubbing trenches for himself, as though he meant to sit down there to the very end of time. He was slow, but much more wary than the world had been led to expect, and he kept convoys tucked in and shielded his slow marching infantry sufficiently well to prevent any heavy adverse scoring.

"But he ought to attack," the young lieutenant had insisted.

"He'll attack us at dawn, somewhere along the lines. You'll get the bayonets coming into the trenches just about when you can see," the war correspondent had held until a week ago.

The young lieutenant winked when he said that.

When one early morning the men the defenders sent to lie out five hundred yards before the trenches, with a view to the unexpected emptying of magazines into any night attack, gave way to causeless panic and blazed away at nothing for ten minutes, the war correspondent understood the meaning of that wink.

"What would you do if you were the enemy?" said the war correspondent, suddenly.

"If I had men like I've got now?"

"Yes."

"Take those trenches."

"How?"

"Oh—dodges! Crawl out half-way at night before moonrise and get into touch with the chaps we send out. Blaze at 'em if they tried to shift, and so bag some of 'em in the daylight. Learn that patch of ground by heart, lie all day in squatty holes, and come on nearer next night. There's a bit over there, lumpy ground, where they could get across to rushing distance—easy. In a night or so. It would be a mere game for our fellows; it's what they're made for...Guns? Shrapnel and stuff wouldn't stop good men who meant business."

"Why don't *they* do that?"

"Their men aren't brutes enough: that's the trouble. They're a crowd of devitalized townsmen, and that's the truth of the matter. They're clerks, they're factory hands, they're students, they're civilized men. They can write, they can talk, they can make and do all sorts of things, but they're poor amateurs at war. They've got no physical staying power, and that's the whole thing. They've never slept in the open one night in their lives; they've never drunk anything but the purest water company water; they've never gone short of three meals a day since they left their feeding bottles. Half their cavalry never cocked leg over horse till it enlisted six months ago. They ride their horses as though they were bicycles—you watch 'em! They're fools at the game, and they know it. Our boys of fourteen can give their grown men points...Very well—"

The war correspondent mused on his face with his nose between his knuckles.

"If a decent civilization," he said, "cannot produce better men for war than—"

He stopped with belated politeness.

"I mean—"

"Than our open-air life," said the young lieutenant, politely.

"Exactly," said the war correspondent. "Then civilization has to stop."

"It looks like it," the young lieutenant admitted.

"Civilization has science, you know," said the war correspondent. "It invented and it makes the rifles and guns and things you use."

"Which our nice healthy hunters and stockmen and so on, rowdy-dowdy cowpunchers, can use ten times better than—*What's that?*"

"What?" said the war correspondent, and then seeing his companion busy with his field-glass he produced his own. "Where?" said the war correspondent, sweeping the enemy's lines.

"It's nothing," said the young lieutenant, still looking.

"What's nothing?"

The young lieutenant put down his glass and pointed. "I thought I saw something there, behind the stems of those trees. Something black. What it was I don't know."

The war correspondent tried to get even by intense scrutiny.

"It wasn't anything," said the young lieutenant, rolling over to regard the darkling evening sky, and generalized, "There never will be anything any more forever. Unless—"

The war correspondent looked inquiry.

"They may get their stomachs wrong, or something—living without proper drains."

A sound of bugles came from the tents behind. The war correspondent slid backward down the sand and stood up. "*Boom!*" came from somewhere far away to the left. "Halloa!" he said, hesitated, and crawled back to peer again. "Firing at this time is jolly bad manners."

The young lieutenant was incommunicative again for a space.

Then he pointed to the distant clump of trees again. "One of our big guns. They were firing at that." he said.

"The thing that wasn't anything?"

"Something over there, anyhow."

Both men were silent, peering through their glasses for a space. "Just when it's twilight," the lieutenant complained. He stood up.

"I might stay here a bit," said the war correspondent.

The lieutenant shook his head. "There is nothing to see," he apologized, and then went down to where his little squad of sun-brown, loose-limbed men had been yarning in the trench. The war correspondent stood up also, glanced for a moment at the business-like bustle below him, gave perhaps twenty seconds to those enigmatic trees again, then turned his face toward the camp.

He found himself wondering whether his editor would consider the story of how somebody thought he saw something black behind a clump of trees, and how a gun was fired at this illusion by somebody else, too trivial for public consultation.

"It's the only gleam of a shadow of interest," said the war correspondent, "for ten whole days."

"No," he said, presently. "I'll write that other article, 'Is War

Played Out?' "

He surveyed the darkling lines in perspective, the tangle of trenches one behind another, one commanding another, which the defender had made ready. The shadows and mists swallowed up their receding contours, and here and there a lantern gleamed, and here and there knots of men were busy about small fires.

"No troops on earth could do it," he said.

He was depressed. He believed that there were other things in life better worth having than proficiency in war; he believed that in the heart of civilization, for all its stresses, its crushing concentrations of forces, its injustice and suffering, there lay something that might be the hope of the world, and the idea that any people by living in the open air, hunting perpetually, losing touch with books and art and all the things that intensify life, might hope to resist and break that great development to the end of time, jarred on his civilized soul.

Apt to his thought came a file of defender soldiers and passed him in the gleam of a swinging lamp that marked the way.

He glanced at their red-lit faces, and one shone out for a moment, a common type of face in the defender's ranks: ill-shaped nose, sensuous lips, bright clear eyes full of alert cunning, slouch hat cocked on one side and adorned with the peacock's plume of the rustic Don Juan turned soldier, a hard brown skin, a sinewy frame, an open, tireless stride, and a master's grip on the rifle.

The war correspondent returned their salutations and went on his way.

"Louts," he whispered. "Cunning, elementary louts. And they are going to beat the townsmen at the game of war!"

From the red glow among the nearer tents came first one and then half-a-dozen hearty voices, bawling in a drawling unison the words of a particularly slab and sentimental patriotic song.

"Oh, *go* it!" muttered the war correspondent, bitterly.

It was opposite the trenches called after Hackbone's Hut that the battle began. There the ground stretched broad and level between the lines, with scarcely shelter for a lizard, and it seemed to the startled, just awakened men who came crowding into the trenches that this was one more proof of that green inexperience of the enemy

5

of which they had heard so much. The war correspondent would not believe his ears at first, and swore that he and the war artist, who, still imperfectly roused, was trying to put on his boots by the light of a match held in his hand, were the victims of a common illusion. Then, after putting his head in a bucket of cold water, his intelligence came back as he toweled. He listened. "Gollys!" he said, "that's something more than scare firing this time. It's like ten thousand carts on a bridge of tin."

There came a sort of enrichment to that steady uproar. "Machine guns!"

Then, "Guns!"

The artist, with one boot on, thought to look at his watch, and went to it hopping.

"Half an hour from dawn," he said. "You were right about their attacking, after all..."

The war correspondent came out of the tent, verifying the presence of chocolate in his pocket as he did so. He had to halt for a moment or so until his eyes were toned down to the night a little. "Pitch!" he said. He stood for a space to season his eyes before he felt justified in striking out for a black gap among the adjacent tents. The artist coming out behind him fell over a tent-rope. It was half-past two o'clock in the morning of the darkest night in time, and against a sky of dull black silk the enemy was talking searchlights, a wild jabber of searchlights. "He's trying to blind our riflemen," said the war correspondent with a flash, and waited for the artist and then set off with a sort of discreet haste again. "Whoa!" he said, presently. "Ditches!"

They stopped.

"It's the confounded searchlights," said the war correspondent.

They saw lanterns going to and fro, near by, and men falling in to march down to the trenches. They were for following them, and then the artist began to feel his night eyes. "If we scramble this," he said, "and it's only a drain, there's a clear run up to the ridge." And that way they took. Lights came and went in the tents behind, as the men turned out, and ever and again they came to broken ground and staggered and stumbled. But in a little while they drew near the crest. Something that sounded like the impact of a very important railway accident happened in the air above them, and the shrapnel bullets seethed about them like a sudden handful of hail. "Right-ho!" said the war correspondent, and soon they judged they had come to the crest and stood in the midst of a world of great darkness and frantic glares, whose principal fact was sound.

Right and left of them and all about them was the uproar, an army-full of magazine fire, at first chaotic and monstrous and then, eked out by little flashes and gleams and suggestions, taking the beginnings of a shape. It looked to the war correspondent as though the enemy must have attacked in line and with his whole force—in which case he was either being or was already annihilated.

"Dawn and the dead," he said, with his instinct for headlines. He said this to himself, but afterward, by means of shouting, he conveyed an idea to the artist.

"They must have meant it for a surprise," he said.

It was remarkable how the firing kept on. After a time he began to perceive a sort of rhythm in this inferno of noise. It would decline—decline perceptibly, droop towards something that was comparatively a pause—a pause of inquiry. "Aren't you all dead yet?" this pause seemed to say. The flickering fringe of rifle flashes would become attenuated and broken, and the *whack-bang* of the enemy's big guns two miles away there would come up out of the deeps. Then suddenly, east or west of them, something would startle the rifles to a frantic outbreak again.

The war correspondent taxed his brain for some theory of conflict that would account for this, and was suddenly aware that the artist and he were vividly illuminated. He could see the ridge on which they stood and before them in black outline a file of riflemen hurrying down towards the nearer trenches. It became visible that a light rain was falling, and farther away towards the enemy was a clear space with men—"our men?"—running across it in disorder. He saw one of those men throw up his hands and drop. And something else black and shining loomed up on the edge of the beam-coruscating flashes; and behind it and far away a calm, white eye regarded the world. "Whit, whit, whit," sang something in the air, and then the artist was running for cover, with the war correspondent behind him. *Bang* came shrapnel, bursting close at hand as it seemed, and our two men were lying flat in a dip in the ground, and the light and everything had gone again, leaving a vast note of interrogation upon the night.

The war correspondent came within bawling range. "What the deuce was it? Shooting our men down!"

7

"Black," said the artist, "and like a fort. Not two hundred yards from the first trench."

He sought for comparisons in his mind. "Something between a big blockhouse and a giant's dish-cover," he said.

"And they were running!" said the war correspondent.

"*You'd* run if a thing like that, searchlight to help it, turned up like a prowling nightmare in the middle of the night."

They crawled to what they judged the edge of the dip and lay regarding the unfathomable dark. For a space they could distinguish nothing, and then a sudden convergence of the searchlights of both sides brought the strange thing out again.

In that flickering pallor it had the effect of a large and clumsy black insect, an insect the size of an ironclad cruiser, crawling obliquely to the first line of trenches and firing shots out of portholes in its side. And on its carcass the bullets must have been battering with more than the passionate violence of hail on a roof of tin.

Then in the twinkling of an eye the curtain of the dark had fallen again and the monster had vanished, but the crescendo of musketry marked its approach to the trenches.

They were beginning to talk about the thing to each other, when a flying bullet kicked dirt into the artist's face and they decided abruptly to crawl down into the cover of the trenches. They had got down with an unobtrusive persistence into the second line, before the dawn had grown clear enough for anything to be seen. They found themselves in a crowd of expectant riflemen, all noisily arguing about what would happen next. The enemy's contrivance had done execution upon the outlying men, it seemed, but they did not believe it would do any more. "Come the day and we'll capture the lot of them," said a burly soldier.

"Them?" said the war correspondent.

"They say there's a regular string of 'em, crawling along the front of our lines...Who cares?"

The darkness filtered away so imperceptibly that at no moment could one declare decisively that one could see. The searchlights ceased to sweep hither and thither. The enemy's monsters were dubious patches of darkness upon the dark, and then no longer dubious, and so they crept out into distinctness. The war correspondent, munching chocolate absent-mindedly, beheld at last a spacious picture of battle under the cheerless sky, whose central focus was an array of fourteen or fifteen huge clumsy shapes lying in perspective on the very edge of the first line of trenches, at intervals of perhaps three hundred yards, and evidently firing down upon the crowded riflemen. They were so close in that the defender's guns had ceased, and only the first line of trenches was in action.

The second line commanded the first, and as the light grew the war correspondent could make out the riflemen who were fighting these monsters, crouched in knots and crowds behind the transverse banks that crossed the trenches against the eventuality of an enfilade. The trenches close to the big machines were empty save for the crumpled suggestions of dead and wounded men; the defenders had been driven right and left as soon as the prow of this land ironclad had loomed up over the front of the trench. He produced his field-glass, and was immediately a center of inquiry from the soldiers about him.

They wanted to look, they asked questions, and after he had announced that the men across the traverses seemed unable to advance or retreat, and were crouching under cover rather than fighting, he found it advisable to loan his glasses to a burly and incredulous corporal. He heard a strident voice, and found a lean and sallow soldier at his back talking to the artist.

"There's chaps down there caught," the man was saying. "If they retreat they got to expose themselves, and the fire's too straight..."

"They aren't firing much, but every shot's a hit."

"Who?"

"The chaps in that thing. The men who're coming up—"

"Coming up where?"

"We're evacuating them trenches where we can. Our chaps are coming back up the zigzags... No end of 'em hit... But when we get clear our turn'll come. Rather! These things won't be able to cross a trench or get into it; and before they can get back our guns'll smash 'em up. Smash 'em right up. See?" A brightness came into his eyes. "Then we'll have a go at the beggar inside," he said.

The war correspondent thought for a moment, trying to realize the idea. Then he set himself to recover his field glasses from the burly corporal.

The daylight was getting clearer now. The clouds were lifting, and a gleam of lemon-yellow amidst the level masses to the east portended sunrise. He looked again at the land ironclad. As he saw it in the bleak gray dawn, lying obliquely upon the slope and on the very lip of the foremost trench, the suggestion of a stranded vessel was very great indeed. It might have been from eighty to a hundred feet long—it was about two hundred and fifty yards away—its vertical side was ten feet high or so, smooth for that height, and then with a complex patterning under the eaves of its flattish turtle cover. This patterning was a close interlacing of portholes, rifle barrels, and telescope tubes—-sham and real—-indistinguishable one from the other. The thing had come into such a position as to enfilade the trench, which was empty now, so far as he could see, except for two or three crouching knots of men and the tumbled dead. Behind it, across the plain, it had scored the grass with a train of linked impressions, like the dotted tracings sea things leave in sand. Left and right of that track dead men and wounded men were scattered—men it had picked off as they fled back from their advanced positions in the searchlight glare from the invader's lines. And now it lay with its head projecting a little over the trench it had won, as if it were a single sentient thing planning the next phase of its attack.

He lowered his glasses and took a more comprehensive view of the situation. These creatures of the night had evidently won the first line of trenches and the fight had come to a pause. In the increasing light he could make out by a stray shot or a chance exposure that the defender's marksmen were lying thick in the second and third line of trenches up towards the low crest of the position, and in such of the zigzags as gave them a chance of a converging fire. The men about him were talking of guns. "We're in the line of the big guns at the crest but they'll soon shift one to pepper them," the lean man said, reassuringly.

"Whup," said the corporal.

"*Bang! bang! bang! Whir-r-r-r!*" It was a sort of nervous jump, and all the rifles were going off by themselves. The war correspondent found himself and the artist, two idle men crouching behind a line of preoccupied backs, of industrious men discharging magazines. The monster had moved. It continued to move regardless of the hail that splashed its skin with bright new specks of lead. It was singing a mechanical little ditty to itself, "*Tuf-tuf, tuf-tuf, tuf-tuf,*" and squirting out little jets of steam behind. It had humped itself up, as a limpet does before it crawls; it had lifted its skirt and displayed along the length of it—*feet!* They were thick, stumpy feet, between knobs and buttons in shape—flat, broad things, reminding one of the feet of elephants or the legs of caterpillars; and then, as the skirt rose higher, the war correspondent, scrutinizing the thing through his glasses again, saw that these feet hung, as it were, on the rims of wheels. His thoughts whirled back to Victoria Street, Westminster, and he saw himself in the piping times of peace, seeking matter for an interview.

"Mr…Mr. Diplock," he said, "and he called them 'pedrails'… Fancy meeting them here!"

The marksman beside him raised his head and shoulders in a speculative mood to fire more certainly—it seemed so natural to assume the attention of the monster must be distracted by this trench before it—and was suddenly knocked backwards by a bullet through his neck. His feet flew up, and he vanished out of the margin of the watcher's field of vision. The war correspondent grovelled tighter, but after a glance behind him at a painful little confusion, he resumed his field glass, for the thing was putting down its feet one after the other, and hoisting itself farther and farther over the trench. Only a bullet in the head could have stopped him looking just then.

The lean man with the strident voice ceased firing to turn and reiterate his point. "They can't possibly cross," he bawled. They—"

"*Bang! Bang! Bang! Bang!*"—drowned everything.

The lean man continued speaking for a word or so, then gave it up, shook his head to enforce the impossibility of anything crossing a trench like the one below, and resumed business once more.

And all the while that great bulk was crossing. When the war correspondent turned his glass on it again it had bridged the trench, and its queer feet were rasping away at the farther bank, in the attempt to get a hold there. It got its hold. It continued to crawl until the greater bulk of it was over the trench—until it was all over. Then it paused for a moment, adjusted its skirt a little nearer the ground, gave an unnerving "*toot, toot,*" and came on abruptly at a pace of, perhaps, six miles an hour straight up the gentle slope towards our observer.

The war correspondent raised himself on his elbow and looked a natural inquiry at the artist.

For a moment the men about him stuck to their position and fired furiously. Then the lean man in a mood of precipitancy slid backwards, and the war correspondent said "Come along" to the artist, and led the movement along the trench.

As they dropped down, the vision of a hillside of trench being rushed by a dozen vast cockroaches disappeared for a space, and instead was one of a narrow passage, crowded with men, for the most part receding, though one or two turned or halted. He never turned back to see the nose of the monster creep over the brow of the trench; he never even troubled to keep in touch with the artist. He heard the "whit" of bullets about him soon enough, and saw a man before him stumble and drop, and then he was one of a furious crowd fighting to get into a transverse zigzag ditch that enabled the defenders to get under cover up and down the hill. It was like a theater panic. He gathered from signs and fragmentary words that on ahead another of these monsters had also won to the second trench.

He lost his interest in the general course of the battle for a space altogether; he became simply a modest egotist, in a mood of hasty circumspection, seeking the farthest rear, amidst a dispersed multitude of disconcerted riflemen similarly employed. He scrambled down through trenches, he took his courage in both hands and sprinted across the open, he had moments of panic when it seemed madness not to be quadrupedal, and moments of shame when he stood up and faced about to see how the fight was going. And he was one of many thousand very similar men that morning. On the ridge he halted in a knot of scrub, and was for a few minutes almost minded to stop and see things out.

The day was now fully come. The gray sky had changed to blue, and of all the cloudy masses of the dawn there remained only a few patches of dissolving fleeciness. The world below was bright and singularly clear. The ridge was not, perhaps, more than a hundred feet or so above the general plain, but in this flat region it sufficed to give the effect of extensive view. Away on the north side of the ridge, little and far, were the camps, the ordered wagons, all the gear of a big army; with officers galloping about and men doing aimless things. Here and there men were falling in, however, and the cavalry was forming up on the plain beyond the tents. The bulk of men who had been in the trenches were still on the move to the rear, scattered like sheep without a shepherd over the farther slopes. Here and there were little rallies and attempts to wait and do—something vague— but the general drift was away from any concentration. There on the southern side was the elaborate lacework of trenches and defenses, across which these iron turtles, fourteen of them spread out over a line of perhaps three miles, were now advancing as fast as a man could trot, and methodically shooting down and breaking up any persistent knots of resistance. Here and there stood little clumps of men, outflanked and unable to get away, showing the white flag, and the invader's cyclist-infantry was advancing now across the open, in open order but unmolested, to complete the work of the machines. Surveyed at large, the defenders already looked a beaten army. A mechanism that was effectually ironclad against bullets, that could at a pinch cross a thirty-foot trench, and that seemed able to shoot out rifle-bullets with unerring precision, was clearly an inevitable victor against anything but rivers, precipices, and guns.

He looked at his watch. "Half past four! Lord! What things can happen in two hours. Here's the whole blessed army being walked over, and at half past two—"

"And even now our blessed louts haven't done a thing with their guns!"

He scanned the ridge right and left of him with his glasses. He turned again to the nearest land ironclad, advancing now obliquely to him and not three hundred yards away, and then scrambled the ground over which he must retreat if he was not to be captured.

"They'll do nothing," he said, and glanced again at the enemy.

And then from far away to the left came the thud of a gun, followed very rapidly by a rolling gunfire.

He hesitated and decided to stay.

The defender had relied chiefly upon his rifles in the event of an assault. His guns he kept concealed at various points upon and behind the ridge ready to bring them into action against any artillery preparations for an attack on the part of his antagonist. The situation had rushed upon him with the dawn, and by the time the gunners had their guns ready for motion, the land ironclads were already in among the foremost trenches. There is a natural reluctance to fire into one's own broken men, and many of the guns, being intended simply to fight an advance of the enemy's artillery, were not in positions to hit anything in the second line of trenches. After that the advance of the land ironclads was swift. The defender-general found himself suddenly called upon to invent a new sort of warfare, in which guns were to fight alone amidst broken and retreating infantry. He had scarcely thirty minutes in which to think it out. He did not respond to the call, and what happened that morning was that the advance of the land ironclads forced the fight, and each gun and battery made what play its circumstances dictated. For the most part it was poor play.

Some of the guns got in two or three shots, some one or two, and the percentage of misses was unusually high. The howitzers, of course, did nothing. The land ironclads in each case followed much the same tactics. As soon as a gun came into play the monster turned itself almost end on, so as to minimize the chances of a square hit, and made not for the gun, but for the nearest point on its flank from which the gunners could be shot down. Few of the hits scored were very effectual; only one of the things was disabled, and that was the one that fought the three batteries attached to the brigade on the left wing. Three that were hit when close upon the guns were clean shot through without being put out of action. Our war correspondent did not see that one momentary arrest of the tide of victory on the left; he saw only the very ineffectual fight of half-battery 96B close at hand upon his right. This he watched some time beyond the margin of safety.

Just after he heard the three batteries opening up upon his left he became aware of the thud of horses' hoofs from the sheltered side of the slope, and presently saw first one and then two other guns galloping into position along the north side of the ridge, well out of sight of the great bulk that was now creeping obliquely towards the crest and cutting up the lingering infantry beside it and below, as it came.

The half-battery swung round into line—each gun describing its curve—halted, unlimbered, and prepared for action.

"*Bang!*"

The land ironclad had become visible over the brow of the hill, and just visible as a long black back to the gunners. It halted, as though it hesitated.

The two remaining guns fired, and then their big antagonist had swung round and was in full view, end on, against the sky, coming at a rush.

The gunners became frantic in their haste to fire again. They were so near the war correspondent could see the expressions on their excited faces through his field-glass. As he looked he saw a man drop, and realized for the first time that the ironclad was shooting.

For a moment the big black monster crawled with an accelerated pace towards the furiously active gunners. Then, as if moved by a generous impulse, it turned its full broadside to their attack, and scarcely forty yards away from them. The war correspondent turned his field glass back to the gunners and perceived it was now shooting down the men about the guns with the most deadly rapidity.

Just for a moment it seemed splendid and then it seemed horrible. The gunners were dropping in heaps about their guns. To lay a hand on a gun was death. "*Bang!*" went the gun on the left, a hopeless miss, and that was the only second shot the half-battery fired. In another moment half-a-dozen surviving artillerymen were holding up their hands amidst a scattered muddle of dead and wounded men, and the fight was done.

The war correspondent hesitated between stopping in his scrub and waiting for an opportunity to surrender decently, or taking to an adjacent gully he had discovered. If he surrendered it was certain he would get no copy off; while, if he escaped, there were all sorts of chances. He decided to follow the gully, and take the first offer in the confusion beyond the camp of picking up a horse.

Subsequent authorities have found fault with the first land ironclads in many particulars, but assuredly they served their purpose on the day of their appearance. They were essentially long, narrow, and very strong steel frameworks carrying the engines, and borne upon eight pairs of big pedrail wheels, each about ten feet in diameter, each a driving wheel and set upon long axels free to swivel round a common axis. This arrangement gave them the maximum of adaptability to the contours of the ground. They crawled level along the ground with one foot high upon a hillock and another deep in a depression, and they could hold themselves erect and steady sideways upon even a steep hillside. The engineers directed the engines under the command of the captain, who had look-out points at small ports all round the upper edge of the adjustable skirt of twelve-inch iron-plating which protected the whole affair, and could also raise or depress a conning tower set about the portholes through the center of the iron top cover. The riflemen each occupied a small cabin of peculiar construction and these cabins were slung along the sides of and before and behind the great main framework, in a manner suggestive of the slinging of the seats of an Irish jaunting-car. Their rifles, however, were very different pieces of apparatus from the simple mechanisms in the hands of their adversaries.

These were in the first place automatic, ejected their cartridges and loaded again from a magazine each time they fired, until the ammunition store was at an end, and they had the most remarkable sights imaginable, sights which threw a bright little camera-obscura picture into the light-tight box in which the rifleman sat below. This camera-obscura picture was marked with two crossed lines, and whatever was covered by the intersection of these two lines, that the rifle hit. The sighting was ingeniously contrived. The rifleman stood at the table with a thing like elaborate draughtsman dividers in his hand, and he opened and closed these dividers, so that they were always at the apparent height—if it was an ordinary-sized man—of the man he wanted to kill. A little twisted strand of wire like an electric-light wire ran from this implement up to the gun, and as the dividers opened and shut the sights went up and down. Changes in the clearness of the atmosphere, due to changes of moisture, were met by an ingenious use of that meteorologically sensitive substance, catgut, and when the land ironclad moved forward the sites got a compensatory deflection in the direction of its motion. The rifleman stood up in his pitch dark chamber and watched the little picture before him. One hand held the dividers for judging distance, and the other grasped a big knob like a door-handle. As he pushed this knob about the rifle above swung to correspond, and the picture passed to and fro like an agitated panorama. When he saw a man he wanted to shoot he brought him up to the cross-lines, and then pressed a finger upon a little push like an electric bell-push, conveniently placed in the center of the knob. Then the man was shot. If by any chance the rifleman missed his target he moved the knob a trifle, or readjusted his dividers, pressed the push, and got him the second time.

This rifle and its sights protruded from a porthole, exactly like a great number of other portholes that ran in a triple row under the eaves of the cover of the land ironclad. Each porthole displayed a rifle and sight in dummy, so that the real ones could only be hit by a chance shot, and if one was, then the young man below said "Pshaw!"

turned on an electric light, lowered the injured instrument into his camera, replaced the injured part, or put up a new rifle if the injury was considerable.

You must conceive these cabins as hung clear above the swing of the axels, and inside the big wheels upon which the great elephant-like feet were hung, and behind these cabins along the center of the monster ran a central gallery into which they opened, and along which worked the big compact engines. It was like a long passage into which this throbbing machinery had been packed, and the captain stood about the middle, close to the ladder that led to his conning tower, and directed the silent, alert engineers—for the most part by signs. The throb and noise of the engines mingled with the reports of the rifles and the intermittent clangor of the bullet hail upon the armor. Ever and again he would touch the wheel that raised his conning tower, step up his ladder until his engineers could see nothing of him above the waist, and then come down again with orders. Two small electric lights were all the illumination of this space—they were placed to make him most clearly visible to his subordinates; the air was thick with the smell of oil and petrol, and had the war correspondent been suddenly transferred from the spacious dawn outside to the bowels of the apparatus he would have thought himself fallen into another world.

The captain, of course, saw both sides of the battle. When he raised his head into his conning tower there were the dewy sunrise, the amazed and disordered trenches, the flying and falling soldiers, the depressed-looking groups of prisoners, the beaten guns; when he bent down again to signal "half speed," "quarter speed," "half circle round towards the right," or what not, he was in the oil-smelling twilight of the ill-lit engine room. Close beside him on either side was the mouthpiece of a speaking-tube, and ever and again he would direct one side or other of his strange craft to "concentrate fire forward on gunners," or to "clear out trench about a hundred yards on our right front."

He was a young man, healthy enough but by no means suntanned, and of a type of feature and expression that prevails in His Majesty's Navy: alert, intelligent, quiet. He and his engineers and his riflemen all went about their work, calm and reasonable men. They had none of that flapping strenuousness of the half-wit in a hurry, that excessive strain upon the blood vessels, that hysteria of effort which is so frequently regarded as the proper state of mind for heroic deeds.

For the enemy these young engineers were defeating they felt a certain qualified pity and a quite unqualified contempt. They regarded these big, healthy men they were shooting down precisely as these same big, healthy men might regard some inferior kind of native. They despised them for making war; despised their bawling patriotisms and their emotionality profoundly; despised them, above all, for the petty cunning and the almost brutish want of imagination their method of fighting displayed. "If they must make war," these young men thought, "why in thunder don't they do it like sensible men?" They resented the assumption that their own side was too stupid to do anything more than play their enemy's game, that they were going to play this costly folly according to the rules of unimaginative men. They resented being forced to the trouble of making man-killing machinery; resented the alternative of having to massacre these people or endure their truculent yappings; resented the whole unfathomable imbecility of war.

Meanwhile, with something of the mechanical precision of a good clerk posting a ledger, the riflemen moved their knobs and pressed their buttons.

The captain of Land Ironclad Number Three had halted on the crest close to his captured half-battery. His lined-up prisoners stood hard by and waited for the cyclists behind to come for them. He surveyed the victorious morning through his conning tower.

He read the general's signals. "Five and Four are to keep among the guns to the left and prevent any attempt to recover them. Seven and Eleven and Twelve, stick to the guns you have got. Seven, get into position to command the guns taken by Three. Then, we're to do something else, are we? Six and One, quicken up to about ten miles an hour and walk round behind that camp to the levels near the river—-we shall bag the whole crowd of them," interjected the young man. "Ah, here we are! Two and Three, Eight and Nine, Thirteen and Fourteen, space out to a thousand yards, wait for the word, and then go slowly to cover the advance of the cyclist infantry against any charge of mounted troops. That's all right. But where's Ten? Halloa! Ten to repair and get movable as soon as possible. They've broken up Ten!"

The discipline of the new war machines was business-like rather than pedantic, and the head of the captain came down out of the conning tower to tell his men. "I say, you chaps there. They've broken up Ten. Not badly, I think; but anyhow, he's stuck."

But that still left thirteen of the monsters in action to finish up the broken army.

The war correspondent stealing down his gully looked back and saw them all lying along the crest and talking, fluttering congratulatory flags to one another. Their iron sides were shining golden in the light of the rising sun.

The private adventures of the war correspondent terminated in surrender about one o'clock in the afternoon, and by that time he had stolen a horse, pitched off it, and narrowly escaped being rolled upon; found the brute had broken its leg, and shot it with his revolver. He had spent some hours in the company of a squad of dispirited riflemen, had quarreled with them about topography at last, and gone off by himself in a direction that should have brought him to the banks of the river and didn't. Moreover, he had eaten all his chocolate and found nothing in the whole world to drink. Also, it had become extremely hot. From behind a broken, but attractive, stone wall he had seen far away in the distance the defender-horsemen trying to charge cyclists in open order, with land ironclads outflanking them on either side. He had discovered that cyclists could retreat over open turf before horsemen with a sufficient margin of speed to allow of frequent dismounts and much terribly effective sharpshooting; and he had a sufficient persuasion that those horsemen, having charged their hearts out, had halted just beyond his range of vision and surrendered. He had been urged to sudden activity by a forward movement of one of those machines that had threatened to enfilade his wall. He had discovered a fearful blister on his heel.

He was now in a scrubby gravelly place, sitting down and meditating on his pocket handkerchief, which had in some extraordinary way become in the last twenty-four hours extremely ambiguous in hue. "It's the whitest thing I've got," he said.

He had known all along that the enemy was east, west, and south of him, but when he heard war Ironclads Numbers One and Six talking in their measured, deadly way not half a mile to the north he decided to make his own little unconditional peace without any further risks. He was for hoisting his white flag to a bush and taking up a position of modest obscurity near it, until someone came along. He became aware of voices, clatter, and the distinctive noises of a body of horse, quite near, and he put his handkerchief in his pocket again and went to see what was going forward.

The sound of firing ceased, and then as he drew near he heard the deep sounds of many simple, coarse, but hearty and noble-hearted soldiers of the old school swearing with vigor.

He emerged from his scrub upon a big level plain, and far away a fringe of trees marked the banks of the river. In the center of the picture was a still intact road bridge, and a big railway bridge a little to the right. Two land ironclads rested, with a general air of being long, harmless sheds, in a pose of anticipatory peacefulness right and left of the picture, completely commanding two miles and more of the river levels. Emerged and halted a few yards from the scrub was the remainder of the defender's cavalry, dusty, a little disordered and obviously annoyed, but still a very fine show of men. In the middle distance three or four men and horses were receiving medical attendance, and nearer a knot of officers regarded the distant novelties in mechanism with profound distaste. Everyone was very distinctly aware of the twelve other ironclads, and of the multitude of townsmen soldiers, on bicycles or afoot, encumbered now by prisoners and captured war gear but otherwise thoroughly effective, who were sweeping like a great net in their rear.

"Checkmate," said the war correspondent, walking out into the open. "But I surrender in the best of company. Twenty-four hours ago I thought war was impossible—and these beggars have captured the whole blessed army! Well! Well!" He thought of his talk with the young lieutenant. "If there's no end to the surprises of science, the civilized people have it, of course. As long as their science keeps going they will necessarily be ahead of open-country men. Still..." He wondered for a space what might have happened to the young lieutenant.

The war correspondent was one of those inconsistent people who always want the beaten side to win. When he saw all these burly, suntanned horsemen, disarmed and dismounted and lined up; when he saw their horses unskillfully led away by the singularly not equestrian cyclists to whom they had surrendered; when he saw these truncated Paladins watching this scandalous sight, he forgot altogether that he had called these men "cunning louts" and wished them beaten not four-and-twenty hours ago. A month ago he had seen that regiment in its pride going forth to war, and had been told of its terrible prowess, how it could charge in open order with each man firing from his saddle, and sweep before it anything else that ever came out to battle in any sort of order, foot or horse. And it had had to fight a few score of young men in atrociously unfair machines!

"Manhood Versus Machinery" occurred to him as a suitable headline. Journalism curdles all one's mind to phrases.

He strolled as near the lined-up prisoners as the sentinels seemed disposed to permit and surveyed them and compared their sturdy proportions with those of their lightly built captors.

"Smart degenerates," he muttered. "Anemic cockneydom."

The surrendered officers came quite close to him presently, and he could hear the colonel's high-pitched tenor. The poor gentleman had spent three years of arduous toil upon the best material in the world perfecting that shooting from the saddle charge, and he was mourning with phrases of blasphemy, natural under the circumstances what one could be expected to do against this suitably consigned ironmongery.

"Guns," said some one.

"Big guns they can walk round. You can't shift big guns to keep pace with them and little guns in the open they rush. I saw 'em rushed. You might do a surprise now and then—assassinate the brutes, perhaps—"

"You might make things like 'em."

"What? *More* ironmongery? Us?"

"I'll call my article," meditated the war correspondent, " 'Mankind Versus Ironmongery,' and quote the old boy at the beginning."

And he was much too good a journalist to spoil his contrast by remarking that the half dozen comparatively slender young men in blue pajamas who were standing about their victorious land ironclad, drinking coffee and eating biscuits, had also in their eyes and carriage something not altogether degraded below the level of a man.

Caught in the Crossfire

DAVID DRAKE

> David Drake studied history, Latin, and law before
> being drafted into the Army in 1970 and
> experiencing South East Asia from the loader's
> hatch of a tank. He is the author of the *Hammer's
> Slammers* series. "Caught in the Crossfire" was
> written in 1978 and originally appeared in *New
> Destinies*, edited by Jim Baen. In 2012, the story
> appeared in the *Mammoth Book of SF Wars*, edited by
> Ian Watson and Ian Whates.

MARGRITTE GRAPPLED with the nearest soldier in the instant
her husband broke for the woods. The man in field gray
cursed and tried to jerk his weapon away from her, but Margritte's
muscles were young and taut from shifting bales. Even when the
mercenary kicked her ankles from under her, Margritte's clamped
hands kept the gun barrel down and harmless.

Neither of the other two soldiers paid any attention to the scuffle.
They clicked off the safety catches of their weapons as they swung
them to their shoulders. Georg was running hard, fresh blood from
his retorn calf muscles staining his bandages. The double slap of wet
automatic fire caught him in mid-stride and whipsawed his slender
body. His head and heels scissored to the ground together. They
were covered by the mist of blood that settled more slowly.

Sobbing, Margritte loosed her grip and fell back on the ground.
The man above her cradled his flechette gun again and looked around
the village. "Well, aren't you going to shoot me, too?" she cried.

"Not unless we have to," the mercenary replied quietly. He was sweating despite the stiff breeze, and he wiped his black face with his sleeve. "Helmuth," he ordered, "start setting up in the building. Landschein, you stay out with me; make sure none of these women try the same damned thing." He glanced out to where Georg lay, a bright smear on the stubbled, golden earth. "Best get that out of sight, too," he added. "The convoy's due in an hour."

Old Leida had frozen to a statue in ankle-length muslin at the first scream. Now she nodded her head of close ringlets. "Myrie, Delia," she called, gesturing to her daughters, "bring brush hooks and come along." She had not lost her dignity even during the shooting.

"Hold it," said Landschein, the shortest of the three soldiers. He was a sharp-featured man who had grinned in satisfaction as he fired. "You two got kids in there?" he asked the younger women. The muzzle of his flechette gun indicated the locked door to the dugout which normally stored the crop out of the sun and heat; today it imprisoned the village's twenty-six children. Delia and Myrie nodded, too dry with fear to speak.

"Then you go drag him into the woods," Landschein said, grinning again. "Just remember—you might manage to get away, but you won't much like what you'll find when you come back. I'm sure some true friend'll point your brats out to us quick enough to save her own."

Leida nodded a command, but Landschein's freckled hand clamped her elbow as she turned to follow her daughters. "Not you, old lady. No need for you to get that near to cover."

"Do you think *I* would run and risk everyone?" Leida demanded.

"Curst if I know what you'd risk," the soldier said. "But we're risking plenty already to ambush one of Hammer's convoys. If anybody gets loose ahead of time to warn them, we can kiss our butts goodbye."

Margritte wiped the tears from her eyes, using her palms because of the gritty dust her thrashings had pounded into her knuckles. The third soldier, the broad-shouldered blond named Helmuth, had leaned his weapon beside the door of the hall and was lifting bulky loads from the nearby air-cushion vehicle. The settlement had become used to whining gray columns of military vehicles, cruising the road at random. This truck, however, had eased over the second canopy of the forest itself. It was a flimsy cargo-hauler like the one in which Krauder picked up the cotton at season's end, harmless enough to look at. Only Georg, left behind for his sickle-ripped leg when a government van had carried off the other males the week before as "recruits", had realized what it meant that the newcomers wore field gray instead of khaki.

"Why did you come here?" Margritte asked in a near-normal voice.

The black mercenary glanced at her as she rose, glanced back at the other women obeying orders by continuing to pick the iridescent boles of Terran cotton grown in Pohweil's soil. "We had the capital under siege," he said, "until Hammer's tanks punched a corridor through. We can't close the corridor, so we got to cut your boys off from supplies some other way. Otherwise the Cartel'll wish it had paid its taxes instead of trying to take over. You grubbers may have been pruning their wallets, but Lord! they'll be flayed alive if your counterattack works."

He spat a thin, angry stream into the dust. "The traders hired us and four other regiments, and you grubbers sank the whole treasury into bringing in Hammer's armor. Maybe we can prove today those cocky bastards aren't all they're billed as..."

"We didn't care," Margritte said. "We're no more the Farm Bloc than Krauder and his truck is the Trade Cartel. Whatever they did in the capital, we had no choice. I hadn't even seen the capital... oh dear Lord, Georg would have taken me there for our honeymoon except that there was fighting all over..."

"How long we got, Sarge?" the blond man demanded from the stark shade of the hall.

"Little enough. Get those bloody sheets set up or we'll have to pop the cork bare-ass naked; and we got enough problems." The big noncom shifted his glance about the narrow clearing, wavering rows of cotton marching to the edge of the forest's dusky green. The road, an unsurfaced track whose ruts were not a serious hindrance to air-cushion traffic, was the long axis. Beside it stood the hall, twenty meters by five and the only above-ground structure in the settlement. The battle with the native vegetation made dugouts beneath the cotton preferable to cleared land wasted for dwellings. The hall became more than a social center and common refectory: it was the gaudiest of luxuries and a proud slap to the face of the forest.

Until that morning, the forest had been the village's only enemy.

"Georg only wanted—"

"God *damn* it," the sergeant snarled. "Will you shut it off? Every man but your precious husband gone off to the siege—no, shut it off till I finish!—and him running to warn the convoy. If you'd wanted to save his life, you should've grabbed him, not me. Sure, all you grubbers, you don't care about the war—not much! It's all one to you whether you kill us yourselves or your tankers do it, those bastards so high and mighty for the money they've got and the equipment. I tell you, girl, I don't take it personal that people shoot at me; it's just the way we both earn our livings. But it's fair, it's even... and Hammer thinks he's the Way made Flesh because nobody can bust his tanks."

The sergeant paused and his lips sucked in and out. His thick, gentle fingers rechecked the weapon he held. "We'll just see," he whispered.

"Georg said we'd all be killed in the crossfire if we were out in the fields when you shot at the tanks."

"If Georg had kept his face shut and his ass in bed, he'd have lived longer than he did. Just shut it off!" the noncom ordered. He turned to his blond underling, fighting a section of sponge plating through the door. "Via, Bornzyk!" he shouted angrily. "Move it!"

Helmuth flung his load down with a hollow clang. "Via, then lend a hand! The wind catches these and—"

"I'll help him," Margritte offered abruptly. Her eyes blinked away from the young soldier's weapon where he had forgotten it against the wall. Standing, she far lacked the bulk of the sergeant beside her, but her frame gave no suggestion of weakness. Golden dust soiled the back and sides of her dress with butterfly scales.

The sergeant gave her a sharp glance, his left hand spreading and closing where it rested on the black barrel-shroud of his weapon, "All right," he said, "you give him a hand and we'll see you under cover with us when the shooting starts. You're smarter than I gave you credit."

They had forgotten Leida was still standing beside them. Her hand struck like a spading fork. Margritte ducked away from the blow, but Leida caught her on the shoulder and gripped. When the mercenary's reversed gun-butt cracked the older woman loose, a long strip of Margritte's blue dress tore away with her. "Bitch," Leida mumbled through bruised lips. "You'd help these beasts after they killed your own man?"

Margritte stepped back, tossing her head. For a moment she fumbled at the tear in her dress; then, defiantly, she let it fall open. Landschein turned in time to catch the look in Leida's eyes. "Hey, you'll give your friends more trouble," he stated cheerfully, waggling his gun to indicate Delia and Myrie as they returned gray-faced from the forest fringe. "Go on, get out and pick some cotton."

When Margritte moved, the white of her loose shift caught the sun and the small killer's stare. "Landschein!" the black noncom ordered sharply, and Margritte stepped very quickly towards the truck and the third man struggling there.

Helmuth turned and blinked at the girl as he felt her capable muscles take the windstrain off the panel he was shifting. His eyes were blue and set wide in a face too large-boned to be handsome, too frank to be other than attractive. He accepted the help without question, leading the way into the hall.

The dining tables were hoisted against the rafters. The windows, unshuttered in the warm autumn and unglazed, lined all four walls at chest height. The long wall nearest the road was otherwise unbroken; the one opposite it was pierced in the middle by the single door. In the center of what should have been an empty room squatted the mercenaries' construct. The metal-ceramic panels had been locked into three sides of a square, a pocket of armor open only toward the door. It was hidden beneath the lower sills of the windows; nothing would catch the eye of an oncoming tanker.

"We've got to nest three layers together," the soldier explained as he swung the load, easily managed within the building, "or they'll cut us apart if they get off a burst this direction."

Margritte steadied a panel already in place as Helmuth mortised his into it. Each sheet was about five centimeters in thickness, a thin plate of gray metal on either side of a white porcelain sponge. The girl tapped it dubiously with a blunt finger. "This can stop bullets?"

The soldier—he was younger than his size suggested, no more than eighteen. Younger even than Georg, and he had a smile like Georg's as he raised his eyes with a blush and said, "P-powerguns, yeah; three layers of it ought to... It's light, we could carry it in the truck where iridium would have bogged us down. But look, there's another panel and the rockets we still got to bring in."

"You must be very brave to fight tanks with just—this," Margritte prompted as she took one end of the remaining armor sheets.

"Oh, well, Sergeant Counsel says it'll work," the boy said enthusiastically. "They'll come by, two combat cars, then three big trucks, and another combat car. Sarge and Landschein buzzbomb the lead cars before they know what's happening. I reload them and they hit the third car when it swings wide to get a shot. Any shooting the blower jocks get off, they'll spread because they won't know—oh, Cop I said it..."

"They'll think the women in the fields may be firing, so they'll kill us first," Margritte reasoned aloud. The boy's neck beneath his helmet turned brick red as he trudged into the building.

"Look," he said, but he would not meet her eyes, "we got to do it. It'll be fast—nobody much can get hurt. And your... the children, they're all safe. Sarge said that with all the men gone, we wouldn't have any trouble with the women if we kept the kids safe and under our thumbs."

"We didn't have time to have children," Margritte said. Her eyes were briefly unfocused. "You didn't give Georg enough time before you killed him."

"He was..." Helmuth began. They were outside again and his hand flicked briefly towards the slight notch Delia and Myrie had chopped in the forest wall. "I'm sorry."

"Oh, don't be sorry," she said. "He knew what he was doing."

"He was—I suppose you'd call him a patriot?" Helmuth suggested, jumping easily to the truck's deck to gather up an armload of cylindrical bundles. "He was really against the Cartel?"

"There was never a soul in this village who cared who won the war," Margritte said. "We have our own war with the forest."

"They joined the siege!" the boy retorted. "They cared that m-much, to fight us!"

"They got in the vans when men with guns told them to get in," the girl said. She took the gear Helmuth was forgetting to hand to her and shook a lock of hair out of her eyes. "Should they have run? Like Georg? No, they went off to be soldiers; praying like we did that the war might end before the forest had eaten up the village again. Maybe if we were really lucky, it'd end before this crop had spoiled in the fields because there weren't enough hands left here to pick it in time."

Helmuth cleared the back of the truck with his own load and

stepped down. "Well, just the same, your husband tried to hide and warn the convoy," he argued. "Otherwise why did he run"

"Oh, he loved me—you know?" said Margritte. "Your sergeant said all of us should be out picking as usual. Georg knew, he told you, that the crossfire would kill everybody in the fields as sure as if you shot us deliberately. And when you wouldn't change your plan... well, if he'd gotten away you would have had to give up your ambush, wouldn't you? You'd have known it was suicide if the tanks learned that you were waiting for them. So Georg ran."

The dark-haired woman stared out at the forest for a moment. "He didn't have a prayer, did he? You could have killed him a hundred times before he got to cover."

"Here, give me those," the soldier said, taking the bundles from her instead of replying. He began to unwrap the cylinders one by one on the wooden floor. "We couldn't let him get away," he said at last. He added, his eyes still down on his work, "Flechettes when they hit... I mean, sh-shooting at his legs wouldn't, wouldn't have been a kindness, you see?"

Margritte laughed again. "Oh, I saw what they dragged into the forest, yes." She paused, sucking at her lower lip. "That's how we always deal with our dead, give them to the forest. Oh, we have a service: but we wouldn't have buried Georg in the dirt, if... if he'd died. But you didn't care, did you? A corpse looks bad, maybe your precious ambush, your own lives. Get it out of the way, toss it in the woods."

"We'd have buried him afterward," the soldier mumbled as he laid a fourth thigh-thick projectile beside those he had already unwrapped.

"Oh, of *course*," Margritte said. "And me, and all the rest of us murdered out there in the cotton. Oh, you're gentlemen, you are."

"Via!" Helmuth shouted, his flush mottling as at last he lifted his gaze to the girl's. "We'd have b-buried him. I'd have buried him. You'll be safe in here with us until it's all over, and by the Lord, then you can come back with us, too! You don't have to stay here with these hard-faced bitches."

A bitter smile tweaked the left edge of the girl's mouth. "Sure, you're a good boy."

The young mercenary blinked between protest and pleasure, settled on the latter. He had readied all six of the tinned, gray missiles;

now he lifted one of the pair of launchers. "It'll be really quick," he said shyly, changing the subject. The launcher was an arm-length tube with double handgrips and an optical sight. Helmuth's big hands easily inserted one of the buzzbombs to lock with a faint snick.

"Very simple," Margritte murmured.

"Cheap and easy," the boy agreed with a smile. "You can buy a thousand of these for what a combat car runs—Hell, maybe more than a thousand. And it's one for one today, one bomb to one car. Landschein says the crews are just a little extra, like weevils in your biscuit."

He saw her grimace, the angry tensing of a woman who had just seen her husband blasted into a spray of offal. Helmuth grunted with his own pain, his mouth dropping open as his hand stretched to touch her bare shoulder. "Oh, Lord—didn't mean to say... "

She gently detached his fingers. His breath caught and he turned away. Unseen, her look of hatred seared his back. His hand was still stretched toward her and hers towards him, when the door scraped to admit Landschein behind them.

"Cute, oh bloody cute," the little mercenary said. He carried his helmet by its strap. Uncovered, his cropped gray hair made him an older man. "Well, get on with it, boy—don't keep me 'n' Sarge waiting. He'll be mad enough about getting sloppy thirds."

Helmuth jumped to his feet. Landschein ignored him, clicking across to a window in three quick strides. "Sarge," he called, "we're all set. Come on, we can watch the women from here."

"I'll run the truck into the woods," Counsel's voice burred in reply. "Anyhow, I can hear better from out here."

That was true. Despite the open windows, the wails of the children were inaudible in the hall. Outside, they formed a thin backdrop to every other sound.

Landschein set down his helmet. He snapped the safety on his gun's sideplate and leaned the weapon carefully against the nest of armor. Then he took up the loaded launcher and ran his hands over its tube and grips. Without changing expression, he reached out to caress Margritte through the tear in her dress.

Margritte screamed and clawed her left hand as she tried to rise. The launcher slipped into Landschein's lap, and his arm, far swifter, locked hers and drew her down against him. Then the little mercenary himself was jerked upward. Helmuth's hand on his collar first broke Landschein's grip on Margritte, then flung him against the closed door.

Landschein rolled despite the shock and his glance flicked towards his weapon, but between gun and gunman crouched Helmuth, no longer a red-faced boy but the strongest man in the room. Grinning, Helmuth spread fingers that had crushed ribs in past rough and tumbles. "Try it, little man," he said. "Try it and I'll rip your head off your shoulders."

"You'll do wonders!" Landschein spat, but his eyes lost their clave and his muscles relaxed. He bent his mouth into a smile. "Hey, kid, there's plenty of slots around. We'll work out something afterward; no need to fight."

Helmuth rocked his head back in a nod of acceptance with nothing of friendship in it. "You lay another hand on her," he said in a normal voice, "and you'd best have killed me first." He turned his back deliberately on the older man and the nearby weapons. Landschein clenched his left fist once, twice, but then he began to load the remaining launcher.

Margritte slipped the patching kit from her belt pouch. Her hands trembled, but the steel needle was already threaded. Her whipstitches tacked the torn piece top and sides to the remaining material, close enough for decency. Pins were a luxury that a cotton settlement could well do without. Landschein glanced back at her once, but at the same time the floor creaked as Helmuth's weight shifted to his other leg. Neither man spoke.

Sergeant Counsel opened the door. His right arm cradled a pair of flechette guns and he handed one to Helmuth. "Best not to leave it in the dust," he said. "You'll be needing it soon."

"They coming, Sarge?" Landschein asked. He touched his tongue to thin, pale lips.

"Not yet." Counsel looked from one man to the other. "You boys get things sorted out?"

"All green here," Landschein muttered, smiling again but lowering his eyes.

"That's good," the big black sergeant said, "because we got a job to do and we're not going to let anything stop us. Anything."

Margritte was putting away her needle. The sergeant looked at her hard. "You keep your head down, hear?"

"It won't matter," the girl said calmly, tucking the kit away. "The tanks, they won't be surprised to see a woman in here."

"Sure, but they'll shoot your bleeding head off," Landschein snorted.

"Do you think I care?" she blazed back. Helmuth winced at the tone; Sergeant Counsel's eyes took on an undesirable shade of interest.

"But you're helping us," the big noncom mused. He tapped his fingertips on the gun in the crook of his arm. "Because you like us so much?" There was no amusement in his words, only a careful mind picking over the idea, all ideas.

She stood and walked to the door, her face as composed as a priest's at the gravesite. "Have your ambush," she said, "Would it help us if the convoy came through before you were ready for it?"

"The smoother it goes, the faster," Counsel agreed quietly, "then the better for all of you."

Margritte swung the door open and stood looking out. Eight women were picking among the rows east of the hall. They would be relatively safe there, not caught between the ambushers' rockets and the raking powerguns of their quarry. Eight of them safe and fourteen sure victims on the other side. Most of them could have been out of the crossfire if they had only let themselves think, only considered the truth that Georg had died to underscore.

"I keep thinking of Georg," Margritte said aloud. "I guess my friends are just thinking about their children; they keep looking at the storage room. But the children, they'll be all right; it's just that most of them are going to be orphans in a few minutes."

"It won't be that bad," Helmuth said. He did not sound as though he believed it either.

The older children had by now ceased the screaming begun when the door shut and darkness closed in on them. The youngest still wailed and the sound drifted through the open door.

"I told her we'd take her back with us, Sarge," Helmuth said.

Landschein chortled, a flash of instinctive humor he covered with a raised palm. Counsel shook his head in amazement. "You were wrong, boy. Now, keep watching those women or we may not be going back ourselves."

The younger man reddened again in frustration. "Look, we've got women in the outfit now, and I don't mean the rec troops. Captain Denzil told me there's six in Bravo Company alone—"

"Hoo, little Helmuth wants his own girlie friend to keep his bed warm," Landschein gibed.

"Landschein, I—" Helmuth began, clenching his right hand into a ridge of knuckles.

"Shut it off!"

"But, Sarge—"

"Shut it off, boy, or you'll have me to deal with!" roared the noncom. Helmuth fell back and rubbed his eyes. The noncom went on more quietly, "Landschein, you keep your tongue to yourself, too."

Both men breathed deeply, their eyes shifting in concert toward Margritte who faced them in silence. "Helmuth," the sergeant continued, "some units take women, some don't. We've got a few, damned few, because not many women have the guts for our line of work."

Margritte's smile flickered. "The hardness, you mean. The callousness."

"Sure, words don't matter," Counsel agreed mildly. He smiled back at her as one equal to another. "This one, yeah; she might just pass. Via, you don't have to look like Landschein there to be tough. But you're missing the big point, boy."

Helmuth touched his right wrist to his chin. "Well, what?" he demanded.

Counsel laughed. "She wouldn't go with us. Would you, girl?"

Margritte's eyes were flat, and her voice was dead flat. "No," she said, "I wouldn't go with you."

The noncom grinned as he walked back to a window vantage. "You see, Helmuth, you want her to give up a whole lot to gain you a bunkmate."

"It's not like that," Helmuth insisted, thumping his leg in frustration. "I just mean—"

"Oh, *Lord!*" the girl said loudly. "Can't you just get on with your ambush?"

"Well, not till Hammer's boys come through," chuckled the sergeant. "They're so good, they can't run a convoy to schedule."

"S-sergeant," the young soldier said, "she doesn't understand." He turned to Margritte and gestured with both hands, forgetting the weapon in his left. "They won't take you back, those witches out there. The... the rec girls at Base Denzil don't go home—they can't. And you know damned well that s-somebody's going to catch it out there when it drops in the pot. They'll crucify you for helping us set up, the ones that're left."

"It doesn't matter what they do," she said. "It doesn't matter at all."

"Your life matters!" the boy insisted.

Her laughter hooted through the room. "My life?" Margritte repeated. "You splashed all that across the field an hour ago. You didn't give a damn when you did it, and I don't give one now—but I'd only follow you to Hell and hope your road was short."

Helmuth bit his knuckle and turned, pinched over as though he had been kicked. Sergeant Counsel grinned his tight, equals grin. "You're wasted here, you know," he said. "And we could use you. Maybe if—"

"Sarge!" Landschein called from his window. "Here they come."

Counsel scooped up a rocket launcher, probing its breech with his fingers to make finally sure of its load. "Now you keep down," he repeated to Margritte. "Backblast'll take your head off if their shooting don't." He crouched below the sill and the rim of the armor shielding him, peering through a periscope whose button of optical fibers was unnoticeable in the shadow. Faced inwards towards the girl, Landschein hunched over the other launcher in the right corner of the protected area. His flechette gun rested beside him and one hand curved toward it momentarily, anticipating the instant he would raise it to spray the shattered convoy. Between them Helmuth knelt as stiffly as a statue of gray-green jade. He drew a buzzbomb closer to his right knee where it clinked against the barrel of his own weapon. Cursing nervously, he slid the flechette gun back out of the way. Both his hands gripped reloads, waiting.

The cars' shrill whine trembled in the air. Margritte stood up by the door, staring out through the windows across the hall. Dust plumed where the long, straight roadway cut the horizon into two blocks of forest. The women in the fields had paused, straightening to watch the oncoming vehicles. But that was normal, nothing to alarm the khaki men in the bellies of their war cars; and if any woman thought of falling to hug the earth, the fans' wailing too nearly approximated that of the imprisoned children.

"Three hundred meters," Counsel reported softly as the blunt bow of the lead car gleamed through the dust. "Two-fifty," Landschein's teeth bared as he faced around, poised to spring.

Margritte swept up Helmuth's flechette gun and leveled it at waist height. The safety clicked off. Counsel had dropped his periscope and his mouth was open to cry an order. The deafening muzzle blast lifted him out of his crouch and pasted him briefly, voiceless, against the pocked inner face of the armor. Margritte swung her weapon like a flail into a triple splash of red. Helmuth died with only a reflexive jerk, but Landschein's speed came near to bringing his launcher to bear on Margritte. The stream of flechettes sawed across his throat. His torso dropped, headless but still clutching the weapon.

Margritte's gun silenced when the last needle slapped out of the muzzle. The aluminum barrel shroud had softened and warped during the long burst. Eddies in the fog of blood and propellant smoke danced away from it. Margritte turned as if in icy composure, but she bumped the door jamb and staggered as she stepped outside. The racket of the gun had drawn the sallow faces of every woman in the fields.

"It's over!" Margritte called. Her voice sounded thin in the fresh silence. Three of the nearer mothers ran towards the storage room.

Down the road, dust was spraying as the convoy skidded into a herringbone for defense. Gun muzzles searched: the running women; Margritte armed and motionless; the sudden eruption of children from the dugout. The men in the cars waited, their trigger fingers partly tensed.

Bergen, Delia's six-year-old, pounded past Margritte to throw herself into her mother's arms. They clung together, each crooning to the other through their tears. "Oh, we were so afraid!" Bergen said, drawing away from her mother. "But now it's all right." She rotated her head and her eyes widened as they took in Margritte's tattered figure. "Oh, Margi," she gasped, "whatever happened to you?"

Delia gasped and snatched her daughter back against her bosom. Over the child's loose curls, Delia glared at Margritte with eyes like a hedge of pikes. Margritte's hand stopped halfway to the child. She stood—gaunt, misted with blood as though sunburned. A woman who had blasted life away instead of suckling it. Delia, a frightened mother, snarled at the killer who had been her friend.

Margritte began to laugh. She trailed the gun three steps before letting it drop unnoticed. The captain of the lead car watched her approach over his gunsights. His short, black beard fluffed out from under his helmet, twitching as he asked, "Would you like to tell us what's going on, honey, or do we got to comb it out ourselves?"

"I killed three soldiers," she answered simply. "Now there's nothing going on. Except that wherever you're headed, I'm going along. You can use my sort, soldier."

Her laughter was a crackling shadow in the sunlight.

Snow in Jerusalem

NATHAN W. TORONTO

Nathan W. Toronto wrote this story in the early 2000s, during the second *intifada* in Israel and the occupied Palestinian territories. He studied Arabic for six months in Jerusalem in college, then spent a year in Cairo studying Arabic before graduate school. One of his favorite jobs was working as an English and Arabic editor for the Carnegie Middle East Center.

I USED TO THINK that snow in Jerusalem was odd, but it has snowed here every winter since peace broke out. At least some call it peace. I call it barely suppressed violence, but it is the closest thing to peace the city has known in recent memory.

There is a State of Palestine, with its capital in the eastern portion of the city, and there are no more suicide bombs or rockets terrorizing the Israelis. There are still knifings and other such attacks, and many people are still fixed on hatred, but the so-called peace has held. For four winters it has held.

Some say that there is a connection between the snow and the peace, that God sent it as punishment. All I know is that I have to walk through it every winter to get to work.

The hill from the Silwan neighborhood, where I used to live, to the Old City—*al-baldeh al-qadeemeh*—is steep. The snow makes it slippery. The sandstone-paved approach to bab al-magharibeh, the closest gate into *al-baldeh*, can be treacherous if the snow melts in the Jerusalem sun then freezes overnight.

If the snow has brought peace, it is not a divine punishment. It is much more personal than that.

I cannot say why we have peace, only why I no longer care for the war. For four years, I have gone to my police job every day, done what they told me, and collected my paycheck. They mostly pay me on time. I do not like dealing with the snow, just like I do not care for Jerusalem-crazed tourists or the Israeli Jews that disrespect me because I am Arab.

I never asked to be a part of the Joint Border Police in *al-baldeh*, but the politicians signed the peace deal, and they agreed that there would be a Joint Border Police. I speak passable English, and I am registered as a Christian, so I was told that if I wanted to keep a government job in Palestine, I had to work in the JBP.

It is not always helpful to be a Christian in Palestine.

All communication in the JBP is in English. They say that this makes it easier for Palestinians and Israelis to cooperate, but after four years of working with the Israelis, in English, I do not believe that speaking in English makes it easier. But I don't care, as long as I can provide for my wife and children. In the fifth year after peace, I got a new Israeli partner, Avi ben Shlomo. He is an annoyance, like the snow, that I tolerate. He probably shot at some relative of mine during the last *intifada*. Maybe he was even the one who shot my cousin in the leg in ar-Ram. My cousin spent a week in Hadasseh Hospital, and still walks with a limp. My partner is about the right age to have done his army service then, and he mentioned once that he served in the West Bank. He calls it Judea and Samaria.

The similarity in our names is a cruel irony. I am Ibrahim. He is Avraham. To avoid thinking about how we have the same name, he calls me Abu Sami, since my eldest son is Sami. I call him Avi, but only to his face and to my superiors. Depending on the Palestinians with whom I am speaking, I call him "my Israeli partner" or "my co-worker" or—if it is someone who might have a connection to Hamas—"the Jews." I do not hate him—I am a Christian, so I hate no one—but I do find it difficult to tolerate him.

One morning, in the fifth year after peace, I trudged up the hill to *bab al-magharibeh*. I made it all the way up the hill and through the gate into *al-baldeh*, and stood in the security line to enter the plaza beneath al-Aqsa Mosque, the place the Israeli Jews call *ha-kotel*. The wait was long, and after I got through, in my haste to get to work, I slipped on the icy sandstone.

Embarrassed, I picked myself up, brushed the mud off my wet rump, and hurried across the plaza, more careful now about my footing. I headed to my assigned station in the Armenian Quarter. I heard snickers from black-clad Jews on the way. I do not understand much Hebrew, but it's easy to tell when people make fun of you.

The snickering did not stop when I got to work. Hamzeh, a Palestinian from Ramallah, and Abdullah, an Israeli Arab, were the only other Arabs I worked with, and neither of them had arrived at the station yet.

The three Jewish police officers at the station broke into broad smiles when I passed by. I could tell that Yitzhak fought to keep down a laugh. "What happen to you, Abu Sami?"

Yitzhak was a peacenik, and I knew he intended no malice, so I ignored him.

Yo'av, though, he rarely had a kind word for us Arabs. He nodded in my direction and smirked. "The snow is wet, no?"

Avi, my partner, shook his head and kept smiling, which made my blood rise. Hamzeh and Abdullah arrived just at that moment. They did not smile. They saw my serious face. Then Yitzhak and Yo'av stopped smiling, and Avi began to cast nervous looks from them to us and back. Thick tension filled the air, like bedouin coffee poured into tiny porcelain cups, full of stickiness and steam.

Would Hamzeh and Abdullah think the Israelis were harassing me? This would create problems for all of us, so I forced myself to chuckle a little bit. At that, the other five began laughing, all a little uneasy. I sighed with relief. No need to endanger my job over some wet pants.

After the laughter died down and the moment passed, Yitzhak gave a fake smile and asked in his optimistic, peacenik voice, "Who is in charge this week?"

We all gathered around the schedule on the wall. I shivered a bit from the cold. Yo'av looked at the schedule and said, in his harsh voice, "Abu Sami this week."

Hamzeh put his hands on his hips and asked, in his English learned in an UNRWA school in Am'ari Camp, "When will this silly rule end, with Arab and Jew change to be in charge each week?"

"It depends," Abdullah said, "on whether one can bear to have the other in charge all the time."

Yo'av turned a cold eye on Abdullah, his disdain for the Israeli Arab plain. "Or if the Arabs can bear to have the Jews in charge?"

Hamzeh moved closer to Abdullah. His eyebrow curled up in challenge. "Jews in charge all times."

Another uncomfortable silence filled the station. Would we ever tire of this tension?

Yo'av's nostrils flared. He was always quickest to anger. Until the peace, his family had lived in a settlement outside Ariel, which is now in Palestine. He says there are probably Arabs living in his house now.

I glared at Hamzeh. He returned my glare at first, but then his face softened. "I'm sorry," he said, and sighed. "My brother hit by car last night, and it having Israeli plates. They did not find responsible one."

"I hope he will be all right," said Yitzhak, a hand on Hamzeh's shoulder.

I breathed easy again, even though there was much left unsaid. The driver of the car could have been a *hamsawi*—a Hamas terrorist—posing as an Israeli, getting at Hamzeh's family for his work. It could have been a radical Israeli settler, trying to create havoc between Palestinians and Israelis. The fact of the matter was that Hamzeh's family might never find justice, but we couldn't worry about that in the JBP.

We had a rule to help avoid tension: no one should say anything accusatory. This was not a JBP rule, this was our rule, among the six of us. Hamzeh broke it and, thankfully, he retracted his comment before it was too late. This rule did more to help Jews and Arabs cooperate than the silly rule that said we should always speak English.

Before we went on patrol, Avi motioned me into the back room. The other four had already left.

What now?

When we got to the back room, to my great surprise he held up a pair of his clean, dry pants. "They probably do not fit, but they are dry."

I gave him a questioning glance, and he continued, "I have a spare uniform here, just in case." Avi lived in the Armenian Quarter, so it was never any trouble for him to take bundles to and from home, since he didn't have to go through a checkpoint. His family had probably long ago displaced some non-Jewish family in order to live in *al-baldeh*, but I tried not to think about it. Given the circumstances, I wasn't in a position to express my annoyance.

"Why you do this?" I asked. My surprise was genuine. I did not think that my Israeli partner cared about my well being.

He laughed a little, "My friends will laugh at me because my station commander wet his pants."

I kicked myself. How silly of me to think he actually cared.

We went out on patrol. A chill stood on the winter air.

Later that week, I returned the so-called favor, without meaning to. It began snowing again, and we stood watch at Damascus Gate, looking for suspicious people going in or out. Yo'av and Hamzeh were stationed on the battlements above the gate, looking at those leaving, and Avi and I stood just outside the dog-leg in the Gate, our eyes scanning those flowing into *al-baldeh* from the steps cascading down from Sultan Suleiman Street.

Our two Jewish-Arab partner teams had been switching posts all day, and the light from the setting sun, purple behind gray clouds, began to recede from the plaza between New Gate and Damascus Gate.

A wrinkled old man hobbled up to us with the patient determination that marks the aged in this part of the world. His knowing gaze fixed on Avi, and it spoke volumes. He could tell that I was an Arab and my partner was a Jew, even though we were both dressed in identical uniforms and body armor and carried identical weapons.

He sneered at Avi, sixty-five years of wizened venom in his eyes. "*Qird yahudi.*"

I could tell that Avi did not understand the Arabic: "Jewish monkey." Still, Avi heard the hatred in the old man's voice. Avi's face grew red, and anger brewed in his eyes. He blew threatening clouds of steam towards the old man.

Then the old man spat in Avi's face. Instinctively, I reached out to grasp Avi's arm, knowing that this old man wanted only to provoke a disproportionate reaction. I also did not want to see this old man, who probably enjoyed great respect among his friends and family, mishandled by an Israeli Jew. "No, Avi. No."

Avi's head whipped around, his glare on me. Steaming spit dripped down his cheek. I took my own handkerchief from my pocket and offered it to him.

"He wants you hit him," I said.

Maybe it was because I was in command that week, or because the man was old and mostly harmless, or because we had learned over and over again in our training that violence in cases like this was not useful. But Avi did not hit the man, or shove him, but I was sure he wanted to. I would have wanted to.

Avi shouted something at the man in fast Hebrew, right in the old man's face. I decided then and there not to note the incident in the day's report. The old man stood there, that determined hatred on his face.

People stopped, tourists, merchants, and beggars. A crowd formed. The tension rose, so I put my arm in front of Avi, my back to the old man, breaking the space between them. A vein on Avi's neck stood out, prominent.

"No, Avi," I said.

Behind the anger in Avi's eyes, I saw fear. How must it have been for Avi, a lone Jew at the main entrance to the Muslim Quarter, with none but a Christian Arab to rely on for support? I scanned the crowd of onlookers. There were probably people there who would do Avi harm, in the right circumstances.

I did not worry for Avi's safety, because the cameras had good sight lines here, but I couldn't let Avi escalate the situation. I did not want his fear to do violence that would only serve those who wanted this peace to fail. This would only make life worse for people like me, for my family.

I kept my arm in front of him, my eyes on him, as calm as I could force myself to be. My other hand, the one on my weapon, trembled violently.

Then I heard a crack, and sharp pain seared through my arm. I whirled to find the source.

The old man had brought his cane down on the middle of my forearm, his undeterred hatred now fixed on me. "'Amil," he said. The calm in his voice stood in odd contrast to the fire in his eyes. "Collaborator."

Me, a collaborator? The insult "collaborator" was reserved for the lowest of the low in Palestinian society, those who sold out family and friends to the Zionists. Collaborators were dragged out into the street and shot, their bodies hung in prominent places to deter any who were contemplating a similar plan. It was even illegal in Palestine to pass information to the Israeli government, even though this law was rarely enforced officially. I myself fought the Zionists in my youth. No, I could not be a collaborator.

My temper got the better of me. I screamed at the man, in Arabic, and forgot all deference to his years. I stabbed my finger into my own chest. "Who organized the Silwan boys to throw stones at the Zionist soldiers during the *intifada*? Me! When Zionist tanks rolled into Nablus, who helped organize the march to *al-baldeh*? Me! Who went to an Israeli prison for demonstrating against the occupation? Me! And you accuse me of being a collaborator? Impossible!"

Then, as suddenly as the man approached, he turned and hobbled off, leaning on his cane. He managed the steps to Sultan Suleiman Street with that same determination.

The crowd's interest waned and they dispersed, leaving Avi and me to stand there, half-stunned from anger and bewilderment. I rubbed my arm, and he breathed deeply.

As if the episode had been a dream, I returned to my post at the opposite side of the archway from Avi. Silent, we waited for the final change of guard before going home for the day. I would also have to forget to put my shouting in Arabic in the report.

At least my arm did not feel broken.

A few days later, I got a taste of what my Israeli partner might have felt that day. He and I manned the checkpoint halfway up the ramp leading from the Jewish kotel plaza to al-Aqsa Mosque. Wet snow slumped to the ground. We had to watch our footing in the slush that settled on the sandstone pavement. I was alone at the metal detector after my partner went to huddle with the x-ray technician over a bag check. Yitzhak, the Israeli peacenik who had volunteered—volunteered!—for the JBP, and Hamzeh, the Muslim from the West Bank, checked documents ten meters farther down the ramp.

I did not see the Haredi Jew before it was too late. I never found out why the guards at the ramp entrance let a Jew onto al-Aqsa without telling us. The Haredim rarely went to al-Aqsa. Haredim used to be forbidden from al-Aqsa. Their presence taunted the Muslim Arabs, but they had as much right as the Muslims to be there, and there were JBP officers posted every thirty or forty meters on al-Aqsa itself, so their security was not as pressing a concern as it used to be.

The Haredi rushed at me, his huge fur hat set snug on his head and his black overcoat swirling about him. Instinctively, I gripped my M-4 carbine tighter as he approached. I tried to bring it up, but I was too tense and too slow. The alarm on the metal detector went off and a glint of metal flashed from his swishing overcoat.

I tried to step out of the way, but I slipped on the slick stone walkway. I was fortunate, for my body fell as the knife came up, and the knife nicked my shoulder instead of plunging into my gut.

Luckily, Avi was more aware than me. As the knife whooshed past by my flailing body, Avi's Tazer popped. The attacker fell, and I felt the burn of the wound in my shoulder. Still, it was better than being poked in the gut. I pressed my glove to my shoulder and breathed a sigh of relief.

After some investigation, we eventually found out that the Haredi wasn't a Haredi at all, but one of the radical settler Jews. I wasn't sure if he knew Yo'av or not, but I didn't want to know, because that might make me suspicious of Yo'av, and suspicions in the Joint Border Police lead to discord, and discord created problems.

I'm not sure why Avi saved my life, since I'd always thought he was as indifferent towards me as I was towards him. Perhaps I was wrong.

Near the end of that winter, I realized that peace was here to stay. How much the snow made this so, I could not decide. It was probably a coincidence. One thing is for certain: the connection between Avi and me became stronger.

One Friday afternoon, about five centimeters of snow sat on the ground. Our whole squad—Yitzhak, Avi, Yo'av, Abdullah, Hamzeh, and I—were on riot duty outside the Franciscan Bible School, second stop on the Via Dolorosa, just inside St. Stephen's Gate. The Friday *khutba*, or sermon, was about to end at al-Aqsa, and we wanted to make sure that those leaving al-Aqsa by way of the Martyrs' Cemetery exited through St. Stephen's Gate instead of coming back into *al-baldeh* to make trouble.

Males aged 13 to 60 were not allowed onto al-Aqsa during Friday prayers, but they still congregated at the Martyrs' Cemetery. We didn't want any trouble, so we six JBP officers stood outside the Franciscan Bible School.

We were not sure how long the khutba would last, and the conversation between us turned odd.

"You know what they say about the snow?" asked Abdullah, the Israeli Arab, in his perfect English.

No one answered, because we all knew Abdullah would answer the question for us. He always did when he had that quirky grin on his face. "Aliens altered the atmosphere to make it snow."

Out of politeness we said nothing, because he said it in a way that made you think he might actually believe it.

"God is punish us for fight," said Hamzeh.

I interpreted this as code for: "God is punishing the Jews for starting it all." But Hamzeh couldn't say that to us; it would have broken our rule against accusatory speech.

"You're both wrong," said Yitzhak, in his usual Israeli way: practical and blunt. "It's a Zionist cloud seeding experiment gone wrong, back when they thought Israel might lose access to the West Bank aquifer."

Some people in Palestine, like the *hamsawis*, thought that Israel still occupied Palestinian land, but a great many more would believe Yitzhak's story about Zionist cloud seeding.

"I heard it was conspiracy of the Arabs," said Yo'av, mocking Arabs that believed in wild conspiracy theories. We ignored his comment, too.

After a short silence, my partner, Avi, chuckled. "I heard the snow came because it got cold."

We all laughed. Avi and I shared a smile, which was new, and reassuring.

The sound of Muslim worshippers leaving al-Aqsa made us grow alert. If the crowds were chanting, we had to be ready for trouble. If the sound was just a disorganized murmur, our job would be easy.

Chanting pulsed from around the corner, down by St. Anne's Church. I pulled my visor down over my face and drew up my riot shield. The six of us, standing abreast, did not even fill the street underneath the remains of Herod's Antonia Fortress. Straight ahead of us was St. Stephen's Gate. The alcove behind us and to our left held the entrance to the Franciscan Bible School, and about twenty meters in front of us the street opened into the Martyrs' Cemetery. The chanting mass came from there, maybe one hundred and fifty of them. With a sickening feeling I realized that they were organized.

Their numbers were small compared to what they might have been in the years before peace, but an organized crowd was formidable against our small patrol. I had organized such crowds to throw stones at the Zionist occupiers during the *intifada,* so I knew the signs. Figures darted in and out of the crowd, carrying messages or rushing to some errand. A single voice screeched above the rest, leading the chant. Other voices shouted with grim determination, trying to mask themselves in the chanting, but I knew better.

"Be ready," I yelled to the other five JBP officers.

Yo'av called for back-up over the radio.

The chanters threw only regular snowballs at first, but then they put stones inside. When we raised our shields to protect our heads, they aimed for our feet and legs. All the while, the mass of stone throwers slowly drew closer. We took a few steps back, uncertain, until another squad of six policemen came up behind us.

The *pop-pop-pop* of rubber bullets sounded behind us, and then a third patrol arrived.

The crowd of chanters did not disperse, but kept marching towards us, in time to the chant.

We couldn't use tear gas because of the close quarters made by the old fortress overhead. They kept on coming, and our two forces met in front of the entryway to the Franciscan Bible School. The door set into the shallow alcove was shut tight.

We pushed back and beat at the chanters with our clubs. I thought for a moment that we would disperse them, but they found some inner reserve and held. I glanced at Avi. Our faces resolute, we held our own against a larger mass of people, this despite the stones that they threw at us.

Then Avi went down beside me. A stone-thrower got lucky. Our riot gear had few openings big enough for a stone to do much damage, much less knock a man down. But Avi went down, and he did so at the worst possible time: right as the crowd surged against us.

He and I anchored the left flank, so he fell into the Franciscan School's alcove. We pushed back, but the crowd surged again. If I did not jump into the alcove while I still could, the crowd would get him when they pushed us past the alcove. Who knows what they might do to a helpless Israeli Jew who was part of the hated JBP?

I had no great love for Avi. At that moment, all I heard in my mind was the pop of his Tazer, that day on the ramp to al-Aqsa. I jumped into the alcove. Had it not been in the heat of the moment, I might have thought of my family first and not jumped in. Avi would probably be dead today, with his blood on my conscience, had I not. I would probably be dead, too.

I pulled Avi as close to the door of the Franciscan Bible School as I could. The chanters surged past us, cutting Avi and me off from the other JBP officers. Two men with knives squeezed into the alcove, but the shock on their faces said that they did not expect to find me there.

I clubbed one man on the head and dropped him in a heap, then slammed my shield into the face of the other. I looked for more of them to come into the alcove, but all of the others—not two meters away from us—were busy keeping the other officers at bay. The policemen were losing, too, so Avi's and my situation quickly became desperate.

I could have used my sidearm to try and shoot our way out of the crowd, but I only had ten rounds, and it would have created more attention for us than we needed. Other would-be killers would soon push their way through the tightly-packed crowd to get to us.

The only escape was into the Franciscan Bible School, but why should the nuns open the door with a riot going on outside? I banged on the door, and got only echoes in return, even though I knew there was always—always—someone just inside the door.

I banged again, but this time I shouted at the nuns in Arabic to open the door. My sense of urgency spiked when I saw the crowd start to jostle, to open the way for others to get into the alcove, probably more knife-wielding attackers. They would be ready for me this time.

The panic simmered around my eyes. I thought of the Lord's Prayer. I yelled it at the top of my lungs, in Arabic, hoping the nuns would have pity on us.

At "forgive us our debts," the bolt clanked free, so I skipped "forgive our debtors" and shoved our two bodies inside. None too soon, because a ferocious pounding followed the bolt driving home again.

For once, it was helpful to be a Christian in Palestine.

That winter, I passed from the ranks of those who thought the peace would fail to those who wanted it to succeed. This wasn't a conflict between Palestinian Arab and Israeli Jewish tribes, or even between Christians, Jews, and Muslims. This was about living. And snow.

I was a stone-thrower once, but I also saved an Israeli Jew from harm at the hands of a Palestinian mob. An old Arab man and a Settler Jew both attacked me, and an Israeli Jew gave me his trousers and probably saved my life when he did not have to. I'm in too deep to go back to war now, especially after what happened the night after the Franciscan Bible School riot.

I got home from work to find our car packed to the brim with luggage and our front room stuffed with our possessions, mounded up in great piles. My wife handed me a brick, around which was tied a note that called me 'amil and said that we had two days to leave our home for good.

My face paled when I saw how the note was fastened to the brick, held on by a green strip of cloth with white lettering that read, "La illaha illa allah, wa Muhammad rusul allah"—"There is no god but God, and Muhammad is God's prophet." The hamsawis were coming for me and my family.

Later that night, with everyone huddled in bed, I heard a knock at the door. I answered it. Hamas never bothered to knock.

I was surprised to find Avi standing there, a worried look on his face. "You must come now," he said, his voice low and urgent. "The terrorists are coming tonight, not after two days. They put two days on the note to make sure that you and your family would be here, still preparing to leave."

A darkened JBP jeep waited behind him, the engine running. I roused my wife and children and urged them into the jeep, with no choice but to trust my Israeli partner, even though my wife grumbled at me in Arabic about it.

We were not three blocks from our house when a massive explosion shook the ground. The Jeep skipped on the road as the concussion waves hit, and car alarms pierced the night air.

We sped away. Sirens wailed on their way to the scene. My wife just stared straight ahead, and my children whimpered in the back seat. But we were alive.

I can't go back to that neighborhood now, because people know me and because the Hamas car bomb that destroyed our house also damaged many houses on our street. My neighbor's daughter had her legs crushed under a slab of concrete, and she will have to walk with crutches for the rest of her life.

I will never be accepted into that neighborhood again. I brought too much disruption, too much pain. I still live in an Arab neighborhood in East Jerusalem, but I can't tell you where. I still work in the JBP, but I've changed my name to protect my family.

I never would have thrown my lot in with this crazy peace plan if I had known it would end up like this. I blame the snow. I just wanted to mind my own business and take care of my family and stay out of politics, but one simple slip in the Jerusalem snow led me to support the peace.

Am I sure the peace will hold? No. But if this peace comes crashing down then I have much more to lose now than I did before. Maybe there is a link between the snow and the peace, but it's not the one people usually think of.

Skirmish at Heklara

JAMES C. GLASS

James C. Glass is a former physicist and 1990 grand prize winner of the Writers of the Future Contest. "Skirmish at Heklara" was originally published in the September 2011 issue of *Digital Science Fiction* and now appears in a 2020 collection of short stories, *Strange Worlds, Near and Far*.

B LOOD-RED LIGHT spilled on hot faces as the echelon of Drop Probes turned north on final approach. Giant Procirus rose to greet them, to warm the faces of the many that might die that day. The three hundred troops inside the Probes were young, hand-picked and just out of jump school. It was their first day of real combat, not the usual mop-up operation. Strong resistance was expected, and the sharp stench of fear filled their nostrils as they made a final weapons check. They joked nervously about snake odors and made bets as to which squad would make it first to the airfield beyond Heklara. The reptilian invaders who had occupied the Terran colony of Torontos were now in retreat after a three-year war. Payback time had finally arrived.

Velora Nett snapped a black magazine into her MAW-44 and released the safety. The assault module pulled back on her neck, and her spine was hurting. She let out a deep lungful of air with a whoosh, swallowed hard to keep down the contents of a pre-dawn breakfast and tried not to look at the others. *We're all scared shitless,* she thought. *Why can't we admit it?*

"Up and on! Two minutes to drop!" Colonel Teg Andrist walked down the center aisle as they stood up clumsily, turning to present modules for inspection. There was a quick inspection of thrusters and para-sail packs; a word of encouragement, a pat on each helmet. As squad leader, Velora was first in line. With the others watching, Andrist turned her around to face him and put his hands on her shoulders. "Wish your dad was alive to see this. Kick some snake ass today, Corporal!"

"Yes sir!"

He continued down the line. "You are Jump Group One of the Twenty-First Hestidian Airborne Division. You are the best there is!"

"Yes sir!" they all screamed.

"I know this as fact, because I have personally trained all of you. You are the Banchees, and today you will kill Kraa. Let me hear it!"

"Kraaaaaa!" they screamed in unison. For that instant, the fear was gone. In another instant, it would return.

"Load and lock!" Andrist stalked back towards the control room as thirty MAW-44 bolts slammed home. "Drop position—move!"

Clumsily they stood up, leaning forward against the heavy weight of the modules on their backs, hunching over to carefully step down into the drop bay running the entire length of the Probe. They sat down, legs stretched before them.

"Hook up!" Andrist opened the control room door and stood in the doorway, bracing himself. "Thirty seconds to drop!"

Velora plugged in her thruster, clutched her heavy weapon to her and remembered the look on her father's face the day she had graduated. He had come up to the platform, his uniform covered with battle ribbons, eyes glistening as he pinned the hawk and lightning bolts on her lapel. Her brother Tal, dear gentle Tal who should have been there in her place, watched from the audience. He came up afterward to give her a kiss and a hug, and then disappeared into the crowd, away from his father's stern face. She had been given special applause for she was only the third woman to graduate from jump school. Now she wondered if she was the only one left alive. She looked up at Colonel Andrist. *Someday*, she thought, *I will command a drop.*

"Visors down! And kill Kraa!"

The floor dropped from beneath them and a shockwave of air hit their chests as the thrusters came on. Velora swung to her right, taking her central place in the delta-wing formation dropping towards the valley below. They had come out at seven thousand feet, heading north. Low-lying hills were on either side of them, and straight ahead was the village of Heklara, now occupied by retreating Kraa survivors left to protect their last airfield beyond. She counted three Kraa Gull fighters and two S-10 Chugs before the concrete strip was obscured by the village, and then they were coming in low and taking forward fire as the lead unit in, followed by nine other drops. They were The First. Velora felt pride surge within her, even as thermite fire rose to meet their attack.

A human being next to her exploded, spraying Velora with blood and shredded tissue. She gasped, aimed her weapon from the hip and fired a burst towards the Kraa perimeter around the village. Dust swirled from the steel splinters of the Reaper rounds she fired and a reptilian face disappeared in gore. She hit the ground on the run as the thrusters shut down and pounded on the release catch twice before the heavy module popped off, suddenly feeling light and fast and emptying two magazines as she moved forward. The Kraa were falling back towards the colony village they had occupied and a moment later she was chasing them, looking straight ahead, not noticing the spider-traps opening up around them on the hillsides and spilling forth the hundreds of Kraa hidden there. She didn't notice until Reapers and Red-Dots were tearing into her squad from all sides, bodies exploding like bombs or bursting into flames. Everywhere she turned there were Kraa, firing at close range. Everywhere she turned there was carnage, bleeding corpses that were once human beings for whom she was responsible. The Kraa streamed down hillsides from every direction, screaming victory, tearing at torn bodies with sharp claws.

And Velora Nett ran for her life.

She sprinted towards her right, around the base of a hill, shredding two Kraa coming at her and running like she had never run before. In only seconds it was suddenly quiet, except for the pounding of her boots on hard ground. No gunfire, no screams of death, only silence—but when she stopped, she heard the faint shrill victory cries of the Kraa and knew full well what they were doing to the wounded or any other survivors. She ran again, following the line of hills until she could no longer hear the horrible sounds of the Kraa, and hid herself between three large boulders near a summit overlooking the village. Deep in shadow, she cried bitterly. Her comrades were dead—and she had run away.

Night came, blessing her with darkness. Velora ate a cracker, drank some water and listened for the slightest sound. At midnight, she heard something: a scratching on rock and then breathing. She leveled her weapon downhill towards inky darkness, held her breath and watched something crawl towards her. A face. Human. She called out softly, "Over here, quick, in the rocks!"

A boy, younger than herself and smeared with blood and dirt, scrambled up to her and collapsed at her side. "Oh, is it good to find someone else out here. I thought I was all alone." Immediately, with the sound of his voice and his delicate face, he reminded Velora of her younger brother.

"Where did *you* come from? I thought everyone else was dead!"

"I'm radioman for drop four. We got caught right in the middle. About half of our unit pulled back and got away with the rest of the drops, but I was forward with my corporal when the snakes started coming out of the ground all around us. They got the corporal, and I ran like hell. Most of their fire seemed directed towards the first units. Is that where you were?"

"Drop one. I'm Nett. Velora. Corporal. Your radio still work?" She pointed to the mound on his back.

"Haven't used it yet. Think we should try it?"

"No, we'll wait until light. The village is just over the hill, and I want to see what's going on first. You got a name?"

"Private Avan Hansold, ma'am. I've heard about you. Your old man's a general or something."

"Make that Vel or Corporal, Private. I'm not an officer."

Avan grimaced. "Sorry—Corporal."

Velora smiled faintly. "Yes, my father was a general, Gera Twenty-Third Skyhawks Division." *Survived the war only to die of a heart attack,* she thought. *Just as well. Now he doesn't have to know his daughter ran from a fight and left people to die.*

"First ones in on Torontos when the Kraa first invaded in full force. Boy, that must have been something."

"Yeah. Look, we've got to move to the top of the hill and see what's going on. You have maps?"

The boy nodded. "And a recorder. Sure looks bare up there. No cover at all."

"We'll drag some brush up with us, enough to cover up with if a Gull comes over."

They left the rocks and crawled on hands and knees to the top of the hill. There was no dried brush to be found, and they huddled in a shallow depression on the summit. It was totally exposed to view from above as they peered down towards the village. Velora scanned the visible and infrared spectrum with her binoculars, sweeping the valley. Below her, green figures moved on the hillsides, popping into the ground and out of view. In the village, two Chugs were moving into a street facing the valley, and a crude barricade had been restored there. Figures scurried around in the village square and then suddenly came together like a herd of animals being driven. Velora zoomed in with the binoculars and saw a group of adult villagers and children being herded by four Kraa. "Uh oh, they've got civilians rounded up. And the Kraa are going back into their spider traps again. Do they *really* think that can work a second time? What we need to do is call down some microwave and boil those hills."

"So give me a frequency," said Avan.

"No call now. I don't like those civvies being down there. Another attack and they'll all be killed for sure. But set it for thirty-five-fifty-five, and be ready."

"Yes, Corporal."

She looked at Avan over her shoulder. "Call me Vel. Look, we can clean those hills with a call, but I need to see what they're setting up in the village. We've got to get closer, maybe even into town. You with me for that?"

"Not too crazy about it, but you're the corporal."

"Good. Best to move in now and get settled before sunrise. Let's see those maps."

Velora pointed with gloved fingers. "Here, here and here is where they've dug spider traps. We'll want to bracket all these hills. Write down the coordinates now so you'll be ready."

Avan did as he was told, quickly yet carefully. Velora watched him work, struck again by how much he reminded her of her brother: quiet, thoughtful, contemplating his drawings or lost in music, his dream world taking him away from a father who talked only about war. Sweet Tal, who was supposed to be the warrior but couldn't be. And then the Kraa invasion of Torontos Colony had come, and there was a war for a daughter to fight.

It remained to be seen if Velora Nett could be the warrior her father had expected. At the moment, she was filled with doubt.

They crawled back to the base of the hill and circled towards the airfield, staying high enough to see the entire village. Small fires burned along the airfield, dimly lighting a line of Kraa shelters. Guards walked randomly around a trio of Gulls parked nearby, and two missile and Gatling-platformed Chugs blocked the main street of the town. Velora made notes on everything and checked coordinates on Avan's maps before they moved on. They came to a shed at the edge of town, behind a darkened house that had shown lights earlier in the evening after the Kraa had herded the civilians into it. There had been muffled shots, and later the Kraa had left. Something bad had happened in that place, but it was close. They hid in the shed until just before dawn, and then scuttled into the house in hopes of getting a better look at the streets. What they got was a look at another horror of war.

The stench hit them as they entered through the back door of the unlocked building and worked their way cautiously down a darkened hall, past a small kitchen heaped with debris and garbage. They entered a larger room at the front of the house. There were piles of bodies—men, women and children, Torontons, all of them third-wave humans with large, dark eyes engineered especially for the weakly lit planet of a red dwarf. They had come here for a new life and found death instead, their blood now covering the floor and walls and windows of the house.

Avan turned and threw up in one corner of the room. He wretched and wretched until nothing more would come up, then wiped his mouth on his sleeve, ashamed, and moved near Velora, who was at a window facing the street. "Doesn't this have any effect on you, or is it just all in a day's work?" he asked bitterly.

"Lucky all I've had to eat in twelve hours is a cracker. Besides, seeing this makes it easier to kill Kraa when the time comes."

"Yeah? Well, it doesn't help me much, but then I'm not in for life. You career people are hard asses."

Velora looked at him sharply. "You don't know shit, Private. And what did you expect from the Kraa? They happen to be fond of killing, and right now I feel the same way."

"Oh, Jesus," said Avan.

"What the hell did you get into this war for?"

"Nobody asked me. I was drafted."

"Oh. Tough deal. But you and your radio are important to me right now, and I want you sticking it out, okay?"

"I'm still here, aren't I?"

"Get over here by the window, but keep low. There's a Chug up the street that can look right in here. Another one left of me, just sittin' there. We've got to get a message out about those spider traps, so start your recorder. It has to be quick to minimize interception, so set up the transmission for a half-second pulse."

Avan did as he was told. "If they've changed the entry code since yesterday, we're dead." He punched in the code letters, set the beeper to indicate a coming transmission and turned to hand Velora the recorder. She talked into it for nearly a minute, giving the coordinates of the hills, the approximate number of Kraa hidden there, the placement of Chugs in the town and the fact that they had found slaughtered citizens.

They waited. The engine of the Chug up the street suddenly growled into life. Velora peered over the window sill. "They're loading up. Supplies coming out of a house across the street, carried by civilians. Only a few Kraa guards—whoa!" She ducked her head down into the gloom. "Almost saw me. Looked right over here for a second. I see four guards, maybe a dozen civvies."

The radio chirped. Avan checked the return code showing on the display, then jacked in the recorder and with the push of a button transmitted Velora's one-minute message in a single half-second burst. In a few minutes there was another chirp as the return message arrived. Avan listened intently, Velora still watching the street. "Vel, I've got Colonel Andrist here. He says sit tight. They're comin' in at oh-six-hundred, and he's called in a microwave sweep from low orbit at that time."

"Okay, we stick it out here," said Velora. *And do what?* she thought. *How do I make up for running from a battle? Die?*

There was a sound from the kitchen at the back of the house, a rattling sound, and then a crunch, like someone stepping on broken glass. A shadow moved in the gloom of the hallway.

Velora swung the MAW-44 towards the hallway, pressing her

back against a wall. "Avan, stay right where you are."

His eyes were the size of a credit coin.

The shadow came slowly down the hall and paused at the edge of the room. Large, liquid eyes gleamed dully in the pre-dawn glow. A tiny girl stood there, barefoot, filthy dress brief enough to show dirty arms and pencil-thin legs. Her thumb was in her mouth and she looked straight at Velora, considering her for a moment, and then she walked over to the far corner of the room to rummage around under a pile of broken bodies. She pushed and tugged at something, and came up with a blond-haired doll covered with blood. She hugged it to herself, and looked at Velora again with huge eyes.

"Oh my God," said Velora. "That must have been her mother."

The little girl started back towards the kitchen, but stopped when Velora beckoned to her. "Come here, darlin'. I'm a friend, and we won't hurt you. Do you want something to eat? Here." Velora took a ration bar out of her pocket and held it out to the girl. The child hesitated for an instant, then walked boldly over to Velora and took the bar from her hand. Only at that instant did her thumb come out of her mouth — she tore the wrapper off with her teeth and began to eat. Velora stroked her hair, smiling at Avan. "Tough little kid, a real survivor. How long you been in here, hon'?"

The child remained silent and the ration bar disappeared quickly. She stood there waiting for more, and Velora fumbled in her pack. "Can you talk to me?"

"Here," Avan said, and he handed a ration bar over to the child, who took it without looking at him.

Silently, the doll hugged to her breast, eyes never leaving Velora's face, the little girl wolfed down the second ration bar. Velora sat the child down on the floor next to her and peeked out the window again. "Still loading. More guards now. I think they're getting ready to move out."

She checked her watch. "Less than an hour until the attack and all we can do is sit here."

"That's just fine with me," Avan said, a little too loudly for Velora's peace of mind. "All this draftee wants is to get home alive."

"And I don't? That's pretty stupid, private." Velora kept the tone of her voice amiable. "I think the only difference between us is commitment."

"Maybe. I don't have to prove anything to anybody in this war.

I serve my time, keep my skin on and go home. You career people, this is your life—all this killing. I think it stinks."

"Keep it down," Velora said, staring at him coldly. "You think it's all about killing, is that it? Well, let me tell you, Private, this is my first major combat mission and I'm just as scared as you are, but I'm never going to get ahead in any game if I'm dead. As far as proving myself, I didn't do very well at that when I ran away from the fight yesterday," she whispered sharply.

Avan's cynical smile vanished in a blink. "Run away? What were you supposed to do, stay there and die? That's not commitment, that's stupid. People were running for their lives all over the place."

"Not corporals," said Velora, looking at the floor.

"Oh shit," mumbled Avan. "I rest my case."

Velora sniffed disdainfully and muffled her voice with a gloved hand. "You remind me of my brother, the would-be artist. Nice, gentle guy who hates everything my father ever stood for and isn't afraid to say so. He was the one who was supposed to be the soldier, not me. But he's not here and I am, and whatever happens, I'll do what I have to do. Got that?"

Seconds stretched to one horrible moment of stunned silence, and then Avan smiled at her sadly, hands playing with the controls on the radio. "Yeah, I've got it. Among my several weaknesses, I also have a big mouth. I'm here too, Vel. I just want to go home alive," he whispered back.

"Okay, then—we just stay here quietly until our people are in the street. There won't be many Kraa out there once the hills are cleaned, but if we're spotted, it only takes one salvo from a Chug and they'll take us home in a bottle. And we've got this little girl here. She understands everything we're saying, you know?" She looked down at the tiny child snuggled against her, a death-grip on the doll with one hand and the thumb of the other firmly locked in a speechless mouth. The pretty head turned again towards the bloody remains in one corner of the room. Velora turned her around, hugged her tightly, looked into those sad, dark eyes and swallowed hard.

"God, Avan," she whispered, "she's only a baby."

Velora checked her watch. Only forty-five minutes until the microwave burn. But from the instant she looked at the watch, it was only fifteen minutes until their own private war with the Kraa began.

In all the horror she had dozed, awakening with a start when Avan prodded her. He was right next to her under the window, whispering frantically into her ear, "Vel, wake up, there's screaming out in the street!"

She jumped to a crouch so quickly that the child nearly fell over, gasping in surprise. It was the first sound she had made. Velora peered over the window sill and saw a small group of civilians in a cluster in the middle of the street, surrounded by six armed Kraa. Women and two older children. The Kraa were poking them with their weapons, moving them across the street in a group and directly towards her hiding place. Down the street, the crew of the idling Chug was climbing up onto the machine and dropping down inside it. Directly in front of her, the engine of the previously silent Chug roared into life, and a snake-like arm reached out to slam shut the entrance hatch. The vehicle lurched forward and rolled quickly down the street to her left.

The cluster of terrified civilians drew nearer and Velora could hear the women pleading in their rough, Toronto dialect: "Please, leave us here and save your own lives. Not the children! Please, not the children!" A Kraa growl that was a laugh answered their cries for mercy, and Velora's face flushed with the sudden realization of what was about to take place. This room in which they had hidden themselves would soon be a killing ground again. The Kraa knew their enemy well: to kill civilians in the open would invite an immediate attack by microwave.

"Avan, take the girl to the kitchen and don't fire until I do. They're coming in the front, six of them and a bunch of civvies. Move!"

Avan grabbed the little girl's hand and duck-walked across body parts and the slippery floor, the child stumbling along behind him. They disappeared down the hallway. Velora backed into a corner by the window, the MAW-44 covering the front door.

There were footsteps by the door and hysterical screaming overwhelmed the growls of the Kraa. The door burst open and the civilians piled in, shrieking at the sight of what awaited them. The guards pushed in behind, teeth flashing from thick, reptilian faces. Women and children stumbled to the far corner of the room, huddling there as the guards, backs turned to Velora, raised their weapons, but at that instant one of the children saw her and pointed. All eyes moved towards Velora's grim face and the weapon she held as she snapped it on auto and sprayed the enemy with splinters of death. Four of the Kraa went down on their faces in a pulpy mess, and a five-foot section of wall disappeared in smoke. The fifth guard had stationed himself by the hallway, too close to the civvies for a clean shot, and now he was turning, bringing his weapon to bear on her. There was an explosion from the kitchen, and the Kraa's chest erupted in a fountain of blood and shredded tissue. Avan. First kill.

"Avan!"

"Yo!"

"Take them out back to the shed *now*." Velora jumped up to look outside and stared straight into the face of the sixth Kraa guard, who had remained outside. His claw was a blur, coming straight through the window and grabbing her by the throat, pulling her up on her toes as spots of colorful light danced before her eyes. She rammed the MAW's muzzle up under his chin and emptied the magazine into his nightmarish head.

"Out the back, out the back!" she screeched at the civilians and then coughed, grabbing at her throat to feel where the guard had clawed her.

The little girl darted into the room and threw herself into the arms of one of the women whom she apparently recognized, the woman sweeping her up with a tearful cry. Women and children stampeded down the hall and out the back door. Outside, the Chug that had been passing by had now stopped and was backing up across the street and turning towards her. No rotating turret, but it was quickly coming into position for a shot. Velora sprinted from the room and down the hall, slamming the back door closed as she exited and saw Avan herding the civvies into the nearby shed. "This way!" she called to him, and he ran to follow her as she moved away from the shed. They had gone only twenty yards when the house behind them erupted in a ball of fire and then shattered as flying embers.

Reaper fire ripped the ground around them and Velora cried out as a splinter tore across her left cheek. Avan was right behind her when she went in the front door of a house and straight out the back, temporarily hidden from the view of the advancing Chug. They entered the neighboring house from the back and crouched in the kitchen, Velora pulling the radio from Avan's back. "Tell them what's going on and get help! In a minute, we're outta here!"

Avan was sending frantically when she looked out the front window in time to see the house next door destroyed by withering fire from the Chug, which then turned and headed straight toward them. It pulled up close, nearly on the porch of the building. "Thermite!" Velora screamed. "Lock and load, and get out of here!" She pulled a magazine of Red-Dot thermite cartridges from her belt, slapped it into the MAW and leaped back to the kitchen, where Avan was struggling to load up the radio. "Leave it! Let's go!"

Avan followed her out the door. She turned right and crept up alongside the building. The Chug's rumble vibrated up through the soles of their boots. She turned over her shoulder and mouthed, "Get anybody?"

"Think so," Avan mouthed back.

Velora peered around the corner of the building, pulled back and yelled, "Follow me!"

The explosion was deafening as the Chug fired, but by then they were climbing up onto it and the building they had left disappeared in flames. Velora stuck her MAW muzzle into a forward port and fired three times. Screaming came from inside the chug. "Get the hatch, get the hatch!" she yelled.

Avan scrambled to the top hatch as it popped open, a claw outstretched. He pointed his MAW straight down and emptied the entire magazine of thermite cartridges into the living space of the Chug. Flame shot skyward and the claw disappeared. The machine's surface was suddenly too hot to stand on, but as Avan clambered down he yelled as blood spattered from his left leg below the hip. He fell heavily at Velora's feet. "Oh shit, oh shit, oh shit!" he cried, rolling in the red dirt. A Reaper had hit him from the side at close range, well above the knee.

A Kraa came around the Chug, his eyes turned down to sight on Avan, and Velora shot him with a Red-Dot at point blank range, the heavy body flashing to ashes in seconds.

Flames from Kraa cinders licked at her boots as she stepped around the Chug and saw a wedge formation of infantry moving towards her from the airfield. She emptied the Red-Dot magazine at them, five of the heat-seeking thermite projectiles striking home, but still the line of shrieking creatures came on. One hundred yards away, then seventy, then fifty. She fired furiously, mindlessly, magazine after magazine, then scrabbled at her belt and found nothing there. Avan moaned as she tore his ammunition belt from him and grabbed up his MAW. By the time she aimed it, the nearest Kraa was only twenty yards away. She sprayed their ranks with Red-Dots and Reapers, weapon on full automatic, the Kraa now stumbling over the bodies of their dead but still coming, screaming just as when they had come at her from the hills. Save one round for yourself, she remembered.

As she grabbed her last magazine, the ground around the Kraa erupted in a wall of dirt, pieces of shattered bodies flying in all directions. Two D-7s swooped low overhead, spraying the street with their Gatlings, on course for the airfield and releasing their missiles a second later. Flames from exploding Gulls belched into the sky as the two-place fighters turned and came back to tear up the street one more time. Velora crouched behind the Chug. They passed over her, veering sharply left and right over a burning Chug at the edge of the village. Clouds of steam surged up from the hills, punctuated with small jets she knew were microwaved Kraa exploding like boiling water balloons in their spider traps. Through the roiling steam she saw the APDPs coming in, dropping wave after wave of troops that raced towards her. Only then did she glance up the street, and, seeing no life there, got down on her knees beside Avan.

One leg and side were soaked in blood, and his face was ashen-gray. He mumbled something incoherent and his eyes rolled around, not seeing her. "Avan, they're here, they're here! Hang on!" She slapped his face once, gently, then a second time, hard. "Don't you *dare* die on me now! Don't you DARE!"

Colonel Andrist looked up from a table heaped with paper as Velora entered his Quonset and saluted him smartly. He returned the salute and smiled. "Good to see you alive, Corporal. For a minor operation, this thing turned into quite a mess that could have been avoided with some accurate reconnaissance. Still have all your parts?"

Velora took a deep breath, her intestines a tangled knot sending pain messages to every nerve in her body. "Sir—there's something

I have to tell you, and it's not easy. But I have to do it, sir, with your permission." She clutched at her pants to keep her hands from shaking.

Andrist leaned back in his chair and made a teepee with his hands in front of his mouth. "Go on," he said.

"During the attack yesterday, when we were surrounded and the Kraa were all coming at us from the hills, sir, I—I ran. I ran from the fight, sir. I have no excuse. It was—a reaction. I felt I had to get out of there, and I did."

Andrist chuckled. "Right into the enemy camp, from the sound of it. Bad thing for them." His smile faded as he saw the look on her face. "What's your point, Corporal?"

Velora was near tears. "I acted in a cowardly manner, sir. That's my point." *And that is the end of my career*, she thought.

Andrist sighed. "Tell me what happened. Everything."

And so she told him everything, from the moment she fled until the time she was fighting from behind a burned-out Chug, expecting to die.

"Now, I want you to think about what you just said, and tell me if those were the acts of a coward."

"Sir, I—"

"They were not, Corporal. I had three hundred people in that attack yesterday, and the only reason any of them came back was because the squad leaders knew when to get the hell out of there and stay alive to fight today. That's just smart, Corporal. You stayed alive, and today you engaged the enemy on your own terms. And shot the hell out of them. And saved lives. That's why I'm putting you in for Officers Training School just as soon as I can find the damn form in this mountain of paperwork. Expect your orders to be cut within a week. You have a lot to learn, but you will be one damn fine officer someday. Anything else?"

Velora stared in disbelief. "No, sir. Uh—thank you, sir."

"Good. That private who was with you is outside. I'll decorate the both of you when we get back in orbit." Andrist stood up, reached across the table and touched her bloody cheek. "Nice wound there. Rub a little salt in it, should make an attractive scar. Let the troops know their officer has seen combat. Dismissed."

Velora turned to leave, still stunned as Andrist said softly, "If the General had seen you out there today, he would've bawled like a baby."

Avan was lying on a stretcher near the Quonset, attended by a medic. Velora rushed to him and fell to her knees, shouting at the medic, "Is he all right? Is he all right?"

The medic looked bored. "He's going home. My guess is he's got a five-year limp ahead of him."

"There goes my dancing career," said Avan weakly. "Guess I'll be an architect instead. Hey, look who's here!"

Velora looked up, finding herself surrounded by the group of Torontons they had saved from slaughter. The little girl was with them, and she stepped forward with a shy smile. "Her name is My-reika," one of the women said, "and she wishes to thank you."

The girl put her bloody arms around Velora's neck, and pressed against her.

"Oh, darlin', you're okay, you're okay." Velora hugged the child fiercely, then looked down at Avan's grinning face.

"Tough guy," said Avan.

Velora reached down and squeezed his shoulder. "Yeah. And you, too."

The War Artist

TONY BALLANTYNE

Tony Ballantyne is a British science fiction and fantasy author. Follow him at tonyballantyne.com or on Twitter @TonyBallantyne. His latest novel is *Midway*, about a writer exploring his relationship with his dying father. "The War Artist" originally appeared in *Further Conflicts*, a 2011 anthology edited by Ian Whates.

MY NAME IS BRIAN GARLICK and I carry an easel into battle.

Well, in reality I carry a sketch book and several cameras, but I like to give people a picture of me they can understand.

The sergeant doesn't understand me, though. He's been staring since we boarded the flier in Marseilles. Amongst the nervous conversation of the troops, their high pitched laughter like spumes of spray on a restless sea, he is a half-submerged rock. He's focusing on me with dark eyes and staring, staring, staring. As the sound of the voices fade to leave no sound but the whistle of the wind and the creak of the pink high visibility straps binding the equipment bundles, he's still staring, and I know he's going to undermine me. I've seen that look before, though less often than you might expect. Most soldiers are interested in what I do, but there are always those who seem to take my presence as an insult to their profession. Here it comes...

"I don't get it," he says. "Why do we need a war artist?"

The other soldiers are watching. Eyes wide, breathing fast and shallow, but they've just found something to distract them from the coming fight. Well, I have my audience; it's time to make my pitch to try and get them on my side for the duration of the coming action.

"That's a good question," I reply. I smile, and I start to paint a picture. A picture of the experienced old hand, the unruffled professional.

"Someone once said a good artist paints what can't be painted. Well, that's what a war artist is supposed to do."

"You paint what can't be painted," says the sergeant. It's to his credit he doesn't make the obvious joke. For the moment he's intrigued, and I take advantage of the fact.

"They said Breughel could paint the thunder," I say. "You can paint lightning, sure, but can you make the viewer hear the thunder? Can you make them feel that rumble, deep in their stomach? That's the job of a war artist, to paint what can't be painted. You can photograph the battle, you can show the blood and the explosions, but does that picture tell the full story? I try to capture the excitement, the fear, the terror." I look around the rows of pinched faces, eyes shiny. "I try to show the heroism."

I've composed my picture now, I surreptitiously snap it. That veneer of pride that overlays the hollow fear filling the flier as it travels through the skies.

The sergeant sneers, the mood evaporates.

"What do you know about all that?"

I see the bitter smiles of the other soldiers. So I paint another picture. I lean forward and speak in a low voice.

"I've been doing this for six years. I was in Tangiers after the first Denial of Service attack. I was in Barcelona when the entire Spanish banking system was wiped out; I was in Geneva when the Swiss government network locked. I know what we're flying into, I know what it's like to visit a state targeted by hackers."

There are some approving nods at this. Or is it just the swaying of the craft as we jump an air pocket? Either way, the sergeant isn't going to be convinced.

"Maybe you've seen some action," he concedes. "Maybe you've been shot at. That doesn't make you one of us. You take off the fatigues and you're just another civilian. You won't get jostled in the street back home, or refused service in shops. You won't have people calling you a butcher, when all you've tried to do is defend their country."

This gets the troops right back on his side. I see the memory of the taunts and the insults written on their faces. Too many people were against us getting involved in the Eurasian war; the numbers have grown since the fighting started. There's a cold look in the troops' eyes. But I can calm them, I know what to say.

"That's why the government sent me here. A war artist communicates the emotions their patron chooses. That's why war artists are nearly always to be found acting in an official capacity. I'm here to tell your side of the story, to counteract those images you see on the web."

That's the truth, too. Well, almost the truth. It's enough to calm them down. They're on my side. Nearly all of them, anyway. The sergeant is still not convinced, but I don't think he ever will be.

"I don't like it," he says. "You've said it yourself, what you're painting isn't real war..."

All that's academic now as the warning lights start to flash: orange sheets of fire engulfing the flier's interior. I photograph the scene, dark bodies lost in the background, faces like flame in the foreground, serious, stern, brave faces, awaiting the coming battle. That's the image I will create, anyway.

"Get ready!" calls the sergeant.

There's a sick feeling in my stomach as we drop towards the battle and I wonder, how can I show that?

A shriek of engines, a surge of deceleration and a jolt and we're down and the rear ramp is falling...

We land in a city somewhere in southern Europe. Part of what used to be Italy, I guess. Red bricks, white plaster, green tiles. I hear gunfire, but it's some distance away. I smell smoke, I hear the sound of feet on the metal ramp, the rising howl of the flier's engines as it prepares to lift off again. I see buildings, a narrow road leading uphill to a blue sky and a yellow sun. I smell something amidst the smoke, something that seems incongruous in this battle scene. Something that reminds me of parties and dinners and dates with women. It takes me a moment in all the confusion of movement to realize what it is.

Red wine. It's running down the street. Not a euphemism, there's a lorry at the top of the hill, the front smashed where it's run into a wall, the driver's arm drooping from the open window, the silver clasp of his watch popped open so it hangs like a bracelet. There are jewels of broken glass scattered on the road, diamonds from the windshield, rubies from the truck's lights and emeralds from the broken bottles that are spilling red blood down the street. It's such a striking image that, instinctively, I begin snapping.

The soldiers are flattening themselves against the vine clad walls that border the street, the chameleon material of their suits changing to dusty white, their guns humming as they autoscan the surrounding area. Their half-seen figures are edging their way up and down the hill, changing color, becoming the red of doors and the dusty dark of windows. They're sizing up the area, doing their job, just like me, cameras in my hand, in my helmet, at my belt. Sizing up the scene.

The peacefulness of the street is at odds with the tension we feel, and I need to capture that. The lazy smell of the midday heat mixed with wine. Lemons hanging waxy from the trees leaning over the white walls, paint peeling from window frames. A soldier pauses to touch the petals trailing from a hanging basket and I photograph that.

As if in response to my action, someone opens fire upon us from up the street and there is a whipsnap of movement all around. The sergeant shouts something into a communicator, the flier whines into the air, guns rattling, I see thin wisps of cloud emerge from the doorway of a house up the hill. Someone fired upon us, and now the flier's returned the compliment. Incendiaries, I guess, seeing the orange white sheets that ripple and flicker up the plaster walls of the building.

I snap the picture, but it's not what I'm after; it's too insubstantial. If I were to paint this, the explosion would be much bigger and blooming and orange. It would burst upon the viewer: a heroic response to a cowardly attack.

Then I see the children, and the image I'm forming collapses. Children and women are tumbling from the house. The sound of the flier, the crackle of the flames, they paint a picture in my mind that doesn't involve children. But the truth is unfolding. There were civilians in there! The camera captures their terrified, wide eyed stares, but it can't capture that weeping, keening noise they make.

It can't capture the lurching realization that someone just made a huge mistake.

I see the look on the sergeant's face, that sheer animal joy, and I turn the camera away. That's not what I'm after, but my hand turns back of its own accord. If I had time, I'd try and sketch it right here and now. There is something about the feelings of the moment, getting them down in pencil.

The sergeant sees me looking at him, and he laughs. "So? Innocents get hurt. That's what happens in war."

I make to answer him, but he's concentrating on his console. The green light of the computer screen illuminates his face.

"That's Saint Mark's church at the top of the hill," he says. "There's a square beyond it with a town hall facing it. We occupy those two buildings, we have the high ground."

He runs his finger across the screen.

"Big rooms in there, wide corridors. A good place to make our base."

A woman screams. She's pleading for something. I see a child; I see a lot of blood. A medic is running up, and I photograph that. The gallant liberators, aiding the poor civilians. That's the problem with a simple snap. Taken out of context, it can mean anything.

But that's why I'm here. To choose the context.

We make it to the top of the hill without further incident. The cries of pain are receding from my ears and memory. I focus on the scene at hand.

A wide square, littered with the torn canvas and broken bodies of umbrellas that once shaded cafe patrons. Upturned tables and chairs. Panic spreads fast when people find their mobile phones and computers have stopped working. They've seen the news from other countries; they know that the rioting is not far behind. Across the square, a classic picture: the signs of money and authority, targeted by the mobs. Two banks, their plate glass fronts are smashed open, their interiors peeled inside out in streamers of plastic and trampled circuitry.

The town hall is even worse. It looks like a hollow shell, the anger of the mob has torn the guts out of this place, eviscerated it.

This is what happens when a Denial of Service attack hits, wiping out every last byte of data attached to a country, smoothing the memory stores to an endless sequence of 1's.

Everything—pay, bank accounts, mortgages—wiped out completely. Law and order breaks down, and armies are sent in to help restore order.

That was the line, anyway.

"Funny," says the woman at my side. "We seem to be more intent on securing militarily advantageous positions than in helping the population."

"Shut up, Friis," snaps the sergeant.

"Just making an observation, Sergeant." The woman winks at me.

"Tell you what, Friis, you like making observations so much, why don't you head in there and check it out? "

"Sure," she says, and she looks at me with clear blue eyes. "You coming, painter boy?"

"Call me Brian."

"Aren't you afraid he might get hurt?" laughs the sergeant.

"I'll look after him."

I pat my pockets, checking my cameras, and follow her through the doorway, the glass crunching beneath my feet.

A large entrance hall, the floor strewn with broken china. The rioters haven't been able to get at the ceiling though, and I snap the colorful frescoes that look down upon us. The soldier notices none of this; she's scanning the room, calm and professional. She speaks without looking at me.

"I'm Agnetha."

"Pleased to meet you."

She has such a delightful accent. Vaguely Scandinavian.

I've heard it before.

I see strands of blonde hair curling from beneath her helmet. Her face is slightly smudged, and it makes her look incredibly sexy.

We move from room to room. Everything is in disarray—this place has been stripped and gutted. There's paper and glass everywhere. Everything that could be broken has been broken.

"Always the same," says Agnetha. "The data goes, and people panic. They have no money to buy food, they can't use the phone. They think only of themselves, looting what they can and then barricading themselves into their houses. They steal from themselves, and then we come in and take their country from them."

"I thought we were here to help!"

She laughs at that, and we continue our reconnaissance.

Eventually, it's done. Agnetha speaks into her radio.

"This place is clear."

I recognize the sergeant's voice. "Good. We'll move in at once. There are reports of guerrilla activity down at the *Via Baciadonne*."

"*Baciadonne*." Agnetha smiles at me. "That means *kisses women*."

She's clever as well as pretty. I like that.

The area is quickly secured, which is good because outside the random sound of gunfire is becoming more frequent. I feel the excitement of the approaching battle building in my stomach. The flier comes buzzing up over the roofs, turning this way and that, and I watch the soldiers as they go through the building, filling it with equipment bundled in pink tape.

We find a room with two doors that open out onto a balcony with a view over the city beyond. Agnetha opens the doors to get a better field of fire, then leans against the wall opposite, her rifle slung across her knees. She smiles coquettishly at me.

"Why aren't you taking my picture?" she asks.

I point the camera at her. We both hear it click.

"Are you going to use that?"

"I don't know."

"Keeping it for your private collection?"

She stretches her legs and yawns.

"You don't mind me being attached to your group, then," I say, "not like your sergeant."

She wrinkles her nose.

"He doesn't speak for all of us. I don't agree with everything the government says, either. We're sent out here with insufficient equipment, less back up, and when we get home we're forgotten about at best. I think it's good that we have people like you here."

She frowns. "So tell me, what are you going to paint?"

"Actually, I don't just paint. I use computers, software, all those things. It's all about the final image."

"I understand that. But what are you going to paint?"

I can't keep evading the issue. For all my fine words about reflecting the war as it really is, the sergeant had it right. I'll paint whatever Command wants me to. I like to paint a picture of myself as a bit of a rogue, but, at heart, I know the establishment has me, body and soul.

"I don't know yet. That's why I'm here. I need to experience this place, and then I can try and convey some emotion."

"What emotion?"

"I don't know that, either."

There's a crackle of gunfire, sharp silver, like tins rattling on the floor. I ignore it.

"You're very pretty," I say.

"Thank you." She lowers her eyes in acknowledgment. I like that. She doesn't pretend she isn't pretty; she takes the compliment on its own terms.

"How did you end up in the army?" I ask.

She yawns and stretches.

"I worked in insurance," she says, and it seems all wrong. So drab and everyday. She should have been a model, or a mountaineer, or an artist or something.

"I lost my job when Jutland got hit by the DoS attack. Everything was lost, policies, claims, payroll. The hackers had been feeding us the same worm for months: the backups were totally screwed."

"I'm sorry," I say, and I am. Really sorry. So that's why her accent sounded so familiar. Fortunately, she doesn't seem to notice my reaction.

"Other people had it worse," she shrugs. "We had a garden; we had plenty of canned goods in the house. My mother had the bath filled with water, all the pans and the dishes. We managed okay until your army moved in to restore order."

She seems remarkably unperturbed by the affair.

"So you joined us out of gratitude?" I suggest.

She laughs.

"No, I joined you for security. This way I get to eat and I'm pretty sure that my salary won't be wiped out at the touch of a button. If your army's servers aren't secure, then whose are?"

"Fair enough."

"No, it's not fair. It's just life. Your army wiped out Jutland's data. Just like it did this country's."

I try to look shocked.

"You think that we are responsible for the trouble here?"

"It's an old trick. Create civil unrest and then send in your troops to sort out the problem. You've swallowed up half of Europe that way."

"I don't think it's that well planned," I said, honestly. "I just think that everyone takes whatever opportunity they can when a DoS hits."

As if to underline the point, the staccato rattle of gunfire sounds in the distance.

"Aren't you worried that I will report you?" I ask. "Have you charged with sedition?"

She rises easily to her feet and walks towards me.

"No. I trust you. You have nice eyes."

She's laughing at me.

"Come here," she says. I lean down and she kisses me on the lips. Gently, she pushes my face away. "You're a very handsome man. Maybe later on we can talk properly."

"I'd like that."

She looks back out of the window, checking the area. Little white puffs of cloud drift across the blue sky.

"So, what are you going to paint?" she asks. "The heroic rescuers, making the country safe once more?"

"You're being sarcastic."

"No," she says, and she pushes a strand of blonde hair back up into her helmet. "No. We all do what we must to get by. Tell me, what will you paint?"

"I honestly don't know yet. I'll know it when I see it." I look down into the square, searching for inspiration. "Look at your troop carrier."

She comes to my side. We look at the concrete gray craft, a brutalist piece of architecture sat amongst the elegant buildings of this city.

"Suppose I were to paint that?" I say. "I have plenty of photos, but I need a context, a setting. I could have it swooping down on the enemy! The smoke, the explosions, the bullets whizzing past."

"That's what the army would like…"

"Maybe. How about I paint it with you all seated around the back? That could send a message to the people back home: that even soldiers are human, they sit and chat and relax. Or should I evoke sympathy? Draw the flier all shot up. The mechanics around it, trying to fix it up. One of you being led from the scene, blood seeping from the bandages."

She nods. She understands. Then her radio crackles, and I hear the sergeant's voice.

"Friis! Get down to the flier! We need help bringing equipment inside."

"Coming!"

"I'll tag along," I say.

The whine of the flier is a constant theme; the engines are never turned off. We join the bustle of soldiers around the rear ramp, all busy unloading the pink bound boxes and carrying them into the surrounding buildings.

"What is all that?" I wonder aloud.

"Servers, terminals, NAS boxes," says Agnetha. "I saw this in Jutland. We're establishing a new government in this place."

"Keep it down, Friis," says the sergeant, but without heat. I notice that no one seems to be denying the charge. The head of the soldier behind him suddenly spouts red blood. I'm photographing the scene before I realize what's happening.

"Sniper!"

Everyone is dropping, looking this way and that.

"Up there," shouts someone.

The sergeant is looking at his console, the green light of the screen illuminating his face.

"That's the Palazzo Egizio. The Via Fossano runs behind it."

He's thinking.

"Friis, Delgado, Kenton. Head to the far end of the street. See if you can get into that white building there."

I raise my head to get a better look, and I feel someone push me back down. At the same time there are more shots and I hear a scream. I feel a thud of fear inside me.

Agnetha has been shot.

Shot protecting me.

She's coughing up blood.

"Agnetha," I begin.

"Get back," yells the Sergeant. "You've caused enough trouble as it is."

Agnetha's trying to speak, but there is too much blood. She holds out her hand and I reach for it, but the sergeant knocks it away.

"Let the medic deal with it," he says. "Let someone who should be here deal with it," he adds, nastily.

The other soldiers have located the sniper now, and I'm left to watch as a man kneels next to Agnetha and takes hold of her arm. She looks at me with those brilliant blue eyes, and I don't see her. For a brief moment I see another picture. Blues and greens. Two soldiers: a man and a woman, standing in front of a flier just like the one behind us. They're surrounded by cheering, smiling civilians. A young child comes forward, carrying a bunch of flowers. A thank you from the grateful liberated.

The picture I painted of Jutland.

I push it from my mind, and I see those brilliant blue eyes are already clouding over.

"We all do what we have to do," I whisper. But is that so true? She joined the army so her family could eat. I'm here simply to build a reputation as an artist.

The medic injects her with something. She closes her eyes. The medic shakes his head. I know what that means. The sergeant looks at me.

"I'm sorry," I say.

"So?" he says, "How's that going to help?" He turns away. The others are already doing the same. Dismissing me.

I take hold of Agnetha's hand, feel the pulse fading.

The picture.

I wonder if Agnetha would approve of what I had done. I suspect not. She was too much of a realist.

I included the flier after all. But not taking off, not swooping down from the skies.

No, this was a different picture.

The point of view is from just outside the cockpit, looking in at the pilot of the craft. And here is where we move beyond the subject matter to the artistic vision, because the person flying the craft is not the pilot, but the sergeant.

His face is there, centered on the picture. He's looking out at the viewer, looking beyond the cockpit.

What can he see? The dead children in the square, sheltered by the bodies of their dead parents? We don't know. But that doesn't matter, because there is a clue in the picture. A clue to the truth. One that I saw all the time, but never noticed. It's written across the sergeant's face. Literally.

A reflection in green from the light of the monitor screen, a tracery of roads and buildings, all picked out in pale green letters. Look closely at his cheek and you can just make out the words "Saint Mark's Church." All those names that were supposedly wiped for good by the DoS attack, and yet there they were, still resident in the sergeant's computer. And none of us found that odd at the time. We could have fed that country's data back to it all along, but we chose not to.

They say a picture paints a thousand words.

For once, those words will be mostly speaking the truth.

Wolf Time

Walter Jon Williams is the award-winning author of
over forty volumes of fiction, including the *Dread
Empire's Fall* series and "The Green Leopard Plague,"
which won the Nebula award in 2004. His blog is as
complex and riveting as his fiction prose. "Wolf
Time" was originally published in 2014.

SPEAKERS IN THE HOSPITAL CEILING chimed a series of low,
whispery, synthesized tones, tones scientifically proven to be
relaxing. Reese looked down at the boy in the hospital bed and felt
her insides twist.

The boy was named Steward, and he'd just had a bullet removed
that morning. In the last few days, mad with warrior zen and a
suicidal concept of personal honor, he'd gone kamikaze and blown
up the whole network. Griffith was dead, Jordan was dead, Spassky
was dead, and nobody had stopped Steward until everything in L.A.
had collapsed entirely. He hadn't talked yet to the heat, but he would.
Reese reached for her gun. Her insides were still twisting.

Steward had been lied to and jacked over and manipulated without his knowing it. Mostly it had been his friend Reese who had
done it to him. She couldn't blame him for exploding when he finally
figured out what had happened.

And now this.

Reese turned off the IV monitor so it wouldn't bleep when he
died, and then Steward opened his eyes.

She could see the recognition in his look, the knowledge of what was about to happen. She might have known he wouldn't make it easy.

"Sorry," she said, and raised the gun. What the hell else could she say? *Maybe we can still be friends, after this is over?*

Steward was trying to say something. She felt herself wring out again.

She shot him three times with her silenced pistol and left. The police guards didn't look twice at her hospital coat and ID. Proper credentials had always been her specialty.

CYA. Reese headed for Japan under a backup identity. Credentials her strong suit, as always. On the shuttle she drank a star beast and plugged her seat's interface stud into the socket at the base of her skull.

She closed her eyes and silently projected the latest scansheets onto the optical centers of her brain, and her lips twisted in anger as for the first time she found out what had really gone down, what she'd been a part of.

Alien pharmaceuticals, tonnes of them, shipped down under illegal cover. The network had been huge, bigger than Reese, from her limited perspective, had ever suspected, and now the L.A. heat had everything. Police and security people everywhere, even in the space habitats, were going berserk.

All along, she'd thought it was friends helping friends, but her friends had jacked her around the same way she'd jacked around Steward. The whole trip to L.A. had been pointless—they had been stupid to send her. Killing Steward couldn't stop what was happening, it was all too big. The only way Reese could stay clear was to hide.

She ordered another drink, needing it badly. The shuttle speakers moaned with the same tuneless synthesized chords as had the speakers in the hospital room. The memory of Steward lying in the bed floated in her mind, tangled in her insides.

She leaned back against the headrest and watched the shuttle's wings gather fire.

Her career as a kick boxer ended with a spin kick breaking her nose, and Reese said the fuck with it and went back to light sparring and kung fu. Beating the hell out of herself in training only to have the hell beaten out of her in the ring was not her idea of the good life. She was thirty-six now and she might as well admit there were sports she shouldn't indulge in, even if she had the threadware for them. The realization didn't improve her mood.

Through the window of her condeco apartment, Reese could see a cold wailing northeast wind drive flying white scud across the shallow, reclaimed Aral Sea, its shriek drowning the minarets' amplified call to prayer.

Neither the wind nor the view had changed in months. Reese looked at the gray Uzbek spring, turned on her vid, and contemplated her sixth month of exile.

Her hair was black now, shorter than she'd worn it in a long time. Her fingerprints were altered, as was the bone structure of her face. The serial numbers on her artificial eyes had been changed. However bleak its weather, Uzbekistan was good at that sort of thing.

The last person she'd known who had lived here was Steward. Just before he came to L.A. and blew everything to smithereens.

A young man on the vid was putting himself into some kind of combat suit, stuffing weapons and ammunition into pockets. He picked up a shotgun. Suspenseful music hammered from the speakers.

Reese turned up the sound and sat down in front of the vid.

She had considered getting back into the trade, but it was too early. The scansheets and broadcasts were still full of stories about aliens, alien ways, alien imports. About "restructuring" going on in the policorps who dealt with the Powers. It was strange seeing the news on the vid, with people ducking for cover, refusing statements, the news item followed by a slick ad for alien pharmaceuticals. People were going to trial—at least those who survived were. A lot were cooperating. Things were still too hot.

Fortunately money wasn't a problem. She had enough to last a long time, possibly even forever.

Gunfire sounded from the vid. The young man was in a shootout with aliens, splattering Powers with his shotgun. Reese felt her nerves turn to ice.

The young man, she realized, was supposed to be Steward. She jumped forward and snapped off the vid.

She felt sickened.

Steward had never shot an alien in his life. Reese ought to know.

Fucking assholes. Fucking media vermin.

She reached for her quilted Chinese jacket and headed for the door. The room was too damn small.

She swung the door open with a bang, and a dark-complected man jumped a foot at the sound. He turned and gave a nervous grin.

"You startled me."

He had an anonymous accent that conveyed no particular origin, just the abstract idea of foreignness. He looked about thirty. He was wearing suede pumps that had tabs of velcro on the bottoms and sides for holding onto surfaces in zero gee. His hands were jammed into a gray, unlined plastic jacket with a half-dozen pockets all sealed by velcro tabs. Reese suspected one of his hands of having a weapon in it. He was shivering from cold or nervousness. Reese figured he had just come down the gravity well—he was wearing too much velcro to have bought his clothes on Earth.

Some descendants of the Golden Horde, dressed in Flieger styles imported from Berlin, roared by on skateboards, the earpieces of their leather flying helmets flapping in the wind.

"Been in town long?" Reese asked.

He told her his name was Sardar Chandrasekhar Vivekenanda and that he was a revolutionary from Prince Station. His friends called him Ken. Two nights after their first meeting, she met him in the Natural Life bar, a place on the top story of a large bank. It catered to exiles and featured a lot of mahogany imported at great cost from Central America.

Reese had checked on Ken—no sense in being foolish—and discovered he was who he claimed to be. The scansheets from Prince mentioned him frequently. Even his political allies were denouncing his actions.

"Ram was trying to blame the February Riots on us," Ken told her. "Cheney decided I should disappear—the riots would be blamed on me, and Cheney could go on working."

Reese sipped her mataglap star, feeling it burn its way down her throat as she glanced down through the glass wall, seeing the wind scour dust over the Uzbeks' metal roofs and receiver dishes. She grinned. "So Cheney arranged for you to take the fall instead of him," she said. "Sounds like a friend of humanity to me, all right."

Ken's voice was annoyed. "Cheney knows what he's doing."

"Sure he does. He's setting up his friends. The question is, do *you* know what you're doing?"

Ken's fine-boned hands made a dismissive gesture. "From here I can make propaganda. Cheney sends me an allowance. I've bought a very good communications system."

She turned to him. "You going to need any soldiers in this revolution of yours?"

He shook his head. His lashes were full and black. "I think not. Prince Station is a hundred years old—it's in orbit around Luna, with ready access to minerals, but it cannot compete effectively with the new equipment on other stations. Ram wants to hang on as long as possible—his policy is to loot the economy rather than rebuild. He's guaranteed the loyalty of the stockholders by paying large dividends, but the economy can't support the dividends anymore, and the riots showed he has lost control over the situation. It is a matter of time only. We do not expect the change will be violent—not a military sort of violence, anyway."

"Too bad. I could use a job in someone's foreign legion about now." She glanced up as a group of people entered the bar—she recognized a famous swindler from Ceres named da Vega, his hands and face covered with expensive, glowing implant jewelry that reminded her of fluorescent slime mold. He was with an all-female group of bodyguards who were supposed to stand between him and any Cerean snatch teams sent to bring him to justice. They were all tall and round-eyed—da Vega liked women that way. He'd tried to recruit Reese when they first met. The pay was generous, round-eyed women being rare here, but sexual favors were supposed to be included.

One of *those* jobs, Reese thought. She was tempted to feed him his socks, bodyguards or not, but in the end told him she was used to a better class of employer.

Da Vega turned to her and smiled. Uzbekistan was suddenly far too small a place.

Reese finished her mataglap star and stood. "Let's go for a walk," she said.

"An architecture of liberation," Ken said. "That's what we're after. You should read Cheney's thoughts on the subject."

The night street filled with a welling tide of wind. Its alloy surface reflected bright holograms that marched up and down dark storefronts, advertising wares invisible behind dead glass. The wind howled in the latticework of radio receivers pointed at the sky, through a spiky forest of antennae. A minaret outlined by flashing red strobes speared a sky that glowed with yellow sodium light.

"Liberation," Reese said. "Right."

"Too many closed systems," Ken said. He shrugged into the collar of his new down jacket. "That's the problem with space habitats in general—they strive for closed ecological systems, and then try to close as much of their economy as possible. There's not enough access. I'm a macroeconomist—I work with a lot of models, try to figure out how things are put together—and the most basic obstacle always seems to be the lack of access to data. We've got a solar system filled with corporate plutocracies, all competing with each other, none giving free access to anything they're trying to do. And they've got colonies in other solar systems, and nothing about those gets out that the policorps don't want us to know. The whole situation is far too unstable—it's impossible to predict what's going to happen because the data simply isn't available. Everything's constructed along the lines of the old Orbital Soviet—not even the people who need the information get the access they require.

"Prince Station's main business is processing minerals—that's okay and it's steady, but the prices fluctuate a lot as new mineral sources are exploited in the Belt and elsewhere, and it requires heavy capital investment to keep the equipment up to date. So for the sake of a stable station economy, it would be nice for Prince to develop another, steadier source of export. Biologicals, say, or custom-configured databases. Optics. Wetware. Export genetics. Anything. But it takes time and resources—five years' worth, say—to set something like that up, and there are other policorps who specialize in those areas. We could be duplicating another group's work, and never know it until suddenly a new product comes onto the market and wipes out our five years' investment. All this secrecy is making for unstable economies. Unstable economies make for unstable political situations—that's why whole policorps suddenly go belly-up."

"So you want the policorps to give away their trade secrets."

"I want to do away with the whole *concept* of trade secrets. Ideally, what I'd like to do is create a whole new architecture of data storage and retrieval. Something that's so good that everyone will have to use it to stay competitive, but something that by its very nature prohibits restriction of access."

Reese laughed. The sound echoed from the cold metal street. "You're dreaming."

He gave her a faint smile. "You're right, of course. I'd have to go back two hundred years, right to the beginning of artificial intelligence, and redesign everything from the start. Then maybe I'd have a chance." He shrugged. "Cheney and I have more practical plans, fortunately."

She looked at him. "You remind me of someone I used to know. He wanted to know the truth, just like you. Wanted access."

"Yes?"

The cold wind seemed to cut her to the bone. "He died," she said. "Somebody shot him in a hospital."

Somehow, caught in the warm rush of memory, she had forgot that ending.

"A funny place to get shot," Ken said.

She remembered Steward's last comprehending look, the final words that never came. The northeaster touched her flesh, chilled her heart. The lonely street where they walked suddenly seemed endless, not just a street but the Street, an endless alloy thoroughfare where Reese walked in chill isolation, moving between walls of neon that advertised phantom, unreal comforts. She shivered and took his hand.

Ken's voice was soft, almost drowned by wind. "Were you close?"

"Yes. No." She tossed her head. "I wanted to be a friend, but it would have been bad for business."

"I see."

She tasted bile on her tongue, gazing down the endless gleaming

Street again, the dark people on it who touched briefly and then parted. Sometimes, she thought, she just needed reminding. She wondered what Steward's last words might have been.

A bare yellow bulb marked the door to Ken's apartment building. They entered, the yellow light streaming through the door to reveal the worn furniture, the bright new communications equipment.

"Hey," Reese said, "it's Agitprop Central." She was glad to be out of the wind.

The room blinked to the distant red pulse of the minaret's air-hazard lights. Reese stopped Ken's hand on the light switch, stopped his mouth, every time he tried to talk, with her tongue. She really didn't care if he had someone special back on Prince, preferred this to happen in a certain restrained, ethical silence.

Her nerves were wired for combat and she snapped them on, speeding her perceptions and making everything seem in slow motion, the way his hands moved on her, the susurrus of her own breath, the endless red beat of the strobe that sketched the outlines of his face in the warm darkness. She could hear the bluster of the northeaster outside, the way it knocked at the panes, shrieked around corners, flooded down the long and empty Street outside.

Kept securely outside, at least for this slow-moving, comforting moment of exile.

A day later a maintenance seal blew out on Prince Station and killed sixteen people. Ken was pleased.

"We can do a lot with this," he said. "Demonstrate how the administration's cronies can't even do simple jobs right."

Reese stood by the window, looking out toward the distant brown horizon, tired of Ken's torn wallpaper and sagging furniture. In the distance, foreigners on Bactrian camels pretended they were carrying silk to Tashkent.

"Sabotage, do you think?" she asked, then corrected herself. "Sorry. Destabilization is the proper term, right?"

He sat cross-legged on his chair, watching the screen with an intent, calculating frown. "It could have been us, yes. An effective little action, if it was."

"The people who got killed weren't volunteers, anyway. Not your people."

He grinned in a puzzled way. "No. Of course not."

Reese turned to look at him, folding her arms. "That's what scares me about you idealists. You shoot sixteen people into a vacuum, and it's all for human betterment and the triumph of the revolution, so everything's okay."

Ken squinted as he looked at her against the light. "I'm not sure it's different from what you do."

"I'm a soldier. You're an ideologue. The difference is that you decide who gets killed and where, and I'm the one that has to do it and face the consequences if you're wrong. If it weren't for people like you, I wouldn't be necessary."

"You think this difference somehow makes you less responsible?"

Reese shook her head. "No. But the people I fight—they're volunteers, same as me. Getting paid, same as me. It's clean, very direct. I take the money, do a job. I don't know what it's about often as not. I don't really want to know. If I asked, the people I work for would just lie anyway." She moved to the shabby plush chair and sat, curling one leg under her.

"I fought for humanity once, in the Artifact War. I was on Archangel with Far Jewel, making the planet safe for the Freconomicist cause. Making use of the alien technology we'd stumbled on by accident, all that biochemware the Powers are so good at. It sounded like a noble adventure, but what we were doing was looting alien ruins and stealing from the other policorps. The war blew up, and next I knew I was below the surface in those alien tunnels, and I was facing extermination cyberdrones and tailored bugs with nothing between death and my skin but a very inadequately armored environment suit. And then I got killed."

Ken looked at her with his head cocked to one side, puzzled. "You had clone insurance? This is a different body?"

Anger burned in Reese as she spoke, and she felt it tempering her muscles, turning them rigid.

Remembered dark tunnels, bodies piled in heaps, the smell of fear that burned itself into the fibers of her combat suit, the scent that no amount of maintenance and cleaning would ever remove.

"No. Nothing like that. I did the killing—I killed myself, my personality. Because everything I was, everything I'd learned, was just contributing to help my employers, my officers, and the enemy in their effort to murder me. I had to streamline myself, get rid of everything that didn't contribute in a positive way toward my own physical survival. I became an animal, a tunnel rat. I saw how qualities like courage and loyalty were being used by our bosses to get us killed, and so I became a disloyal coward. My body was working against me—I'm too tall for tunnels—but I tried real hard to get short, and funny enough it seemed to work. Because in times like that, if you've got your head right, you can do what you have to."

She looked at Ken and grinned, baring her teeth. An adrenaline surge, triggered by the violent memory, prickled the down on her arms. "I'm still an animal. I'm still disloyal. I'm still a coward. Because that's the only way to keep alive."

"If you feel that way, you could get out of the business."

She shrugged. "It's what I do best. And if I did something else— got a job as a rigger, or some kind of tech—then I'd just be somebody else's animal, a cow maybe, being herded from one place to another and fed on grass. At least this way, I'm my own animal. I get my reward up front."

"And during?" Ken's dark eyes were intent.

Reese shifted in her seat, felt a certain discomfort. Nerves, she thought, jinking from the adrenaline. "I'm not sure what you mean."

"You like the work. I have that impression."

She laughed. No reason to be defensive about it. "I like being wired and hanging right on the edge. I like knowing that I have to do things right, that any mistake I make matters."

He shook his head. "I don't understand that. People like you."

"You haven't had to become an animal. You're a macroeconomist, and you're trained to take the long view. A few people blown out a hatch, that's just an acceptable sacrifice. I tend to take this kind of thing personally, is all. See, I figure everyone who ever tried to get me killed was looking at the long view."

Ken's gaze was steady. "I'm not planning on getting you killed. That's not part of my view."

"Maybe someday I'll end up standing between you and your revolution. Then we'll see."

He didn't say anything. In the steadiness of his dark eyes, the absence of expression, Reese read her answer, and knew it was the one she'd expected.

"Reese."

It was the first time she'd heard her name in six months, and now it came from a complete stranger on a street corner in Uzbekistan. Her hardwired nerves were triggered and her combat thread was evaluating the man's stance, calculating possible dangers and responses, before she even finished her turn.

He was about forty, tanned, with receding brown hair and a widow's peak. His stance was open, his hands in plain sight: he wore a blue down vest over a plaid shirt, baggy gray wool pants, old brown square-toed boots. He smiled in a friendly way. His build was delicate, as if he'd been genetically altered. His face was turning ruddy in the wind.

"You talking to me?" Reese asked him. "My name's Waldman." Her wetwear was still evaluating him, analyzing every shift in posture, movement of his hands. Had Ken shopped her? she wondered. Had Cheney, after deciding she was a danger to Ken?

His smile broadened. "I understand your caution, but we know who you are. Don't worry about it. We want to hire you."

His voice was as American as hers. Her speeded-up reflexes gave her plenty of time to contemplate his words.

"You'd better call me Waldman if you want to talk to me at all."

He put up his hands. Her nerves crackled. She noticed he had a ragged earlobe, as if someone had torn off an earring in a fight. "Okay, Miss Waldman. My name's Berger. Can we talk?"

"The Natural Life, in an hour. Do you know where that is?"

"I can find out. See you there."

He turned and walked casually up the narrow street. She watched till he was gone and then went to the apartment she rented in a waterfront condecology. She looked for signs anyone had been there in her absence—there weren't any, but that didn't mean anything—and then, to calm her jittery nerves, she cleaned her pistol and took a long, hot bath with the gun sitting on the side of the steel tub. She stretched out as far as the tub would let her, feeling droplets of sweat beading on her scalp while she watched the little bathroom liquid-crystal vidscreen show a bouncy pop-music program from Malaysia. She changed her clothes, put the pistol back in its holster—the security softwear at the Natural Life would shred her with poisoned darts if she tried to carry it in—and then headed back into town.

The muezzins' songs hung in the gusty air. Her mind sifted possibilities.

Berger was the heat. Berger was an assassin. Da Vega had shopped her out of pique. Cheney had sold her name. Ken had regretted telling her so much about his revolution and decided to have her iced before she sold his plans to Ram.

Life was just so full of alternatives.

Berger hadn't arrived at the bar when she came in. The bartender was at prayer and so she turned on the desktop comp and read the scansheets, looking for something that might give her an edge, help her to understand what it was about.

Nothing. The aliens hadn't generated any headlines today. But there was a note about a Cerean exile named da Vega who had been found dead, along with a couple of his bodyguards. Another bodyguard was missing.

Reese grinned. The Uzbeks, a people who usually endorsed the long view, had probably turned da Vega into fertilizer by now.

The amplified muezzins fell silent. The bartender returned and flipped on todo music broadcast by satellite from Japan. He took her order and then Berger walked in, dabbing at his nose with a tissue. He hadn't been ready, he explained, for this bitter a spring. He'd have to buy a warm jacket.

"Don't worry, Miss Waldman," he added. "I'm not here to crease you. If I wanted to do that, I could have done it on the street."

"I know. But you might be a cop trying to lure me out of Uzbekistan. So I hope to hell you can prove to me who you are."

He grinned, rubbed his forehead uncomfortably. "Well. To tell you the truth, I am a policeman, of a sort."

"Terrific. That really makes my day."

He showed her ID. She studied it while Berger went on. "I'm a captain in Brighter Suns' Pulsar Division. We'd like to hire you for a job up the well."

"Vesta?"

"No. Closer to Earth."

Reese frowned. Policorp Brighter Suns was one of the two policorps that had been set up to deal with the alien Powers. It was almost exclusively into Power imports, and its charter forbade it from owning territory outside of its home asteroid, Vesta. A lot of

Brighter Suns execs were running for cover ever since Steward had blown Griffith's network in L.A., and the whole Vesta operation was being restructured.

"The Pulsar Division handles internal security on Vesta," Reese said. "Your outside intelligence division is called Group Seven. So why is Pulsar handling a matter so far away from home?"

"What we'd like you to handle is an internal security matter. Some of our people have gone rogue."

"You want me to bring them back?"

Something twitched the flesh by one of Berger's eyes. She knew what he was going to say before the words came out his mouth. She felt her nerves tingling, her muscles warming. It had been a long time.

"No. We want you to ice them."

"Don't tell me anything more," she said. "I'm going to check you out before I listen to another word."

"It's not even murder, I'd say," Berger said. He was eating spinach salad in an expensive restaurant called the Texas Beef, named after a vaguely pornographic and wildly popular vid show from Alice Springs. Dressing spattered the creamy tablecloth as Berger waved his fork. "We've got tissue samples and memory thread, like we do for all our top people—hell, we'll clone 'em."

"That doesn't mean I can't end up in prison for it."

"Who's gonna catch you? It's a goddam asteroid fifty zillion klicks from anywhere."

She had checked him out as far as she could. After telling him what she was going to do, she'd sent a message to Vesta asking for confirmation of the existence of one Captain Berger of the Pulsar Division, that and a photo. Both arrived within twelve hours. If this was a plot to arrest her, it had some unlikely elements.

Reese took a mouthful of lamb in mustard sauce. She worked out hard enough, she figured, and deserved her pleasures.

"The rock's about two kilometers in diameter. The official name is 2131YA, but it's also called Cuervo Gold."

"Funny names they're giving asteroids these days."

"They've run out of minor Greek gods, I guess. Cuervo's officially owned by a nonpolicorporate mining company called Exeter Associates, which in turn is owned by us. Gold's an Apollo asteroid, crossing Earth's orbit on a regular schedule, and that makes it convenient for purposes of resupply, and also makes it a lot more isolated than any of the rocks in the Belt. We've had a lab there for a while, using it to develop some technology that—" He grinned. "Well, that we wanted to keep far away from any competition. Security on Vesta is tight, but it's a port, people are always coming in and out. What we've got on the asteroid is pretty hot stuff, and we wanted to keep it away from the tourists."

"I don't really want to know," Reese said.

"I don't know myself, so I couldn't tell you," Berger said. "The work was in a fairly advanced stage when certain activities relating to your old friend Griffith became public. It became an urgent matter to shut down the project and transfer its members to other duties in central Africa, where I work. If the investigators found out about our owning that asteroid, and what's on it, Brighter Suns could be very embarrassed."

"The techs refused to move?" Reese asked.

"They protested. They said their work was entering a critical stage. A transport was sent from Earth to pick them up, but they refused to evacuate, and then we lost touch with the freighter. We think the crew have been killed or made prisoner."

"Your people could have defected to another policorp, using the transport."

"We don't think so. Their work would have been hard to take with them. And they couldn't have gone far without attracting attention—some of the lab personnel were Powers."

A coolness moved through Reese's bones. She sat up, regarding Berger carefully. Powers were forbidden off the two entry ports— the official reason was that there was too much danger of cross-contamination from alien life-forms. Plagues had already devastated the two Power legations, and the reverse was always a possibility. The discovery of Powers in Brighter Suns' employ outside of Vesta would ruin Brighter Suns' credit for good.

But after a while the heat on Brighter Suns would die down. Trade with the aliens was too profitable for people to interfere with it for long. In a year or two, the lab could be reopened with cloned personnel and some very mean security goons to make certain they followed orders.

"I understand your sense of urgency," Reese said. "But why me? Why not go yourself?"

"We don't have anyone with your talents on Earth," Berger said. "I'm not wired the way you are. And, well, we'd like to know you're gainfully employed by us rather than floating around Uzbekistan waiting to be captured by the heat. If we can find you, they probably can."

Reese sipped her club soda. "How did you find me, exactly?"

"Someone recognized you."

"Who might that have been?"

The skin by Berger's eye gave a leap. "It's already taken care of," he said. "We didn't want him giving your name to anyone else."

Da Vega.

Well. At least it wasn't Ken.

But there was also a threat: Berger didn't want her in this refugees' paradise, where the number of desperate people was higher than average and where a policorporate kidnap team could find her. If they'd already iced one person, they could put the ice on another.

"Let's talk payment," Reese said. "Brighter Suns, I think, can afford to pay me what I'm worth."

Ram's cops had beaten some woman to death during interrogation. Ken was busy at his console, putting out fact and opinion pieces, making the most of another death for the revolution. Reese paced the room, picking at the tattered wallpaper, eating Mongolian barbecue from a waxed paper container. Below the window, some drunken descendant of the Golden Horde was singing a sad song to the moon. He kept forgetting the lyrics and starting over, and the burbling ballad was getting on Reese's nerves.

"I'd feel better," she said, "if Cheney was paying you a decent wage."

"He pays what he can afford." Ken's fingers sped over his keyboard. "The money has to be laundered, and he has to be careful how he does it."

"You don't even have a promise of a job after it's all over."

Ken shrugged. "Prince can always use another economist."

"And you don't have protection. Ram could order you iced."

"He needs a live scapegoat, not a dead martyr." He frowned as he typed. "This isn't a mysterious business, you know. Ram knows our strength and most of our moves, and we know his. There aren't very many hidden pieces on the board."

The Uzbek began his song again. Reese clenched her teeth. She put her hand on Ken's shoulder.

"I'm disappearing tomorrow," she said.

He tilted his head back, looking up in surprise. His fingers stopped moving on the keys.

"What's wrong?"

"Nothing. I got a job."

She saw a confirmation in his eyes. "Not one you can talk about," he said.

"No. But it's not for Ram. In case you were wondering."

He took her hand in one of his. "I'll miss you."

Reese put her food carton on top of his video display. Her chopsticks jabbed the air like rabbit-ear antennae.

"I've got another twelve hours before I take the plane to Beijing."

Ken turned off his console. "I can send the rest out tomorrow," he said.

Reese was surprised. "What about the revolution?"

He shrugged and kissed the inside of her wrist. "Sometimes I feel redundant. The revolution is inevitable, after all."

"It's nice to know," Reese said, "that the devil can quote ideology to his purpose."

Outside, the Uzbek continued his wail to the desolate stars.

The tug was called *Voidrunner*, and it was thirty years old at least, the padding on its bulkheads patched with silver tape, bundles of cable hanging out of access hatches. Reese had been in enough ships like it not to let the mess bother her—all it meant was that the tug didn't have to impress its passengers. The air inside tasted acrid, as if the place was crammed full of sweating men, but there were only four people on board.

Berger introduced the other three to Reese, then left, waving cheerily over his shoulder. About four minutes later, *Voidrunner* cast off from Charter Station and began its long acceleration to its destination.

Reese watched the departure from the copilot's chair in the armored docking cockpit. The captain performed the maneuvers with his eyes closed, not even looking out the bubble canopy at the silver-bright floodlit skin of Charter, reality projected into his head through his interface thread, his eyelids twitching as his eyes reflexively scanned mental indicators.

His name was Falkland. He was about fifty, an Artifact War veteran who, fifteen years before, had been doing his level best to kill Reese in the tunnels of Archangel. A chemical attack had left his motor reflexes damaged, and he wore a light silver alloy exoskeleton. Fortunately his brain and interface thread had survived the war intact. He wore a gray beard and his hair long over his collar.

"Prepare for acceleration," he said, his eyes still closed. "We'll be at two gees for the first six hours."

Reese looked out at Earth's dull gray moon, vast, taking up most of the sky. "Right," she said. "Got my piss bottle right here." Hard gees were tough on the bladder.

After the long burn *Voidrunner* settled into a constant one-gee acceleration. Falkland stayed strapped in, his eyelids still moving to some internal REM light show. Reese unbuckled her harness, stretched her relieved muscles while her spine and neck popped, and moved downship.

Falkland offered no comment.

The crew compartment smelled of fresh paint. Reese saw the tug's engineer, a tiny man named Chung, working on a bulkhead fire alarm. His head was bobbing to music he was feeding to his aural nerves.

Chung was so into the technophilic Destinarian movement he was turning himself slice by slice into a machine. His eyes were clear implants that showed the interior silver circuitry; his ears were replaced by featureless black boxes, and there were other boxes of obscure purpose jacked into his hairless scalp. His teeth were metal, and liquid-crystal jewelry, powered by nerve circuitry, shone in ever-changing patterns on his cheeks and on the backs of his hands. He hadn't said anything when Berger introduced him, just looked at Reese for a moment, then turned back to his engines.

Now he said something. His voice was hoarse, as if he wasn't used to using it. "He's downship. In Cargo B."

His back was to Reese, and she had been moving quietly. His head still bobbed to inaudible music. He hadn't even turned his head to speak. "Thanks," she said. "Nice implants."

"The best. I built 'em myself."

"Aren't you supposed to be monitoring the burn?"

He pointed at one of his boxes. "I am."

"Nice."

She always found common ground with control freaks.

Vickers was in Cargo B, as Chung had promised. He was Reese's armorer, hired by Berger for the sole purpose of maintaining the combat suit that Reese was to wear on Cuervo. Vickers was young, about eighteen, and thin. His dark hair was cut short; he had a stammer and severe acne. He was dressed in oil-spattered coveralls. When Reese walked in, Vickers was peeling the suit's components out of their foam packing. She helped him lay the suit on the deck. Vickers grinned.

"W-wolf 17," he said. His voice was American Southern. "My favorite. You're gonna kick some ass with this. It's so good it can p-practically do the job by itself."

The suit was black, long-armed, anthropoid. The helmet, horned by radio antennae, was fused seamlessly to the shoulders. Inside, Reese's arms, legs, and body would fit into a complex web that would hold her tightly: the suit would amplify and strengthen her every move. It wasn't entirely natural movement—she'd have to get used to having a lot more momentum in free fall than she normally did.

"F-fuckin' great machine," Vickers said. Reese didn't answer.

The Wolf's dark viewplate gleamed in the cool cabin light. There was a clean functionality to its design that made it even more fearful—nothing in its look gave the impression that it was anything but a tool for efficient murder. The white Wolf trademark shone on the matte-black body of the suit. Reese fought a memory charged with fear—Wolf made most of the cyberdrones she'd encountered on Archangel. The combat suit, free of its packing, had a smell she'd hoped she'd never scent again.

"I want to look at the manual," she said. "And the schematics." If her life was going to depend on this monster, she wanted to know everything there was to know about it.

Vickers looked at her approvingly. "I've got them on thread in m-my cabin. The suit's standard, except for some c-custom thread woven into the t-target acquisition unit. Berger knows who you're going to b-be gunning for, and he put in some specific target identification routines. You're gonna be h-hot."

"That's the plan," Reese said. The smell of the Wolf, oil and plastic webbing and cold laminate armor, rose in her senses. She repressed a shiver.

Vickers was still admiring the Wolf. "One wicked son of a bitch," he said.

When talking to machines, Reese noticed, Vickers lost his stammer.

Reese and the Wolf moved as one in the void. Amber-colored target acquisition data glowed on the interior of the black faceplate. Below them the asteroid glittered as flecks of mica and nickel reflected the relentless sun.

No way they're not gonna know you're coming, Berger had told her. *Not with your ship's torch coming at them. We stabilized the rock's spin, so you can try landing on the blind side, but they're smart enough to have put detectors out there, so we can't count on surprise. What we're going to have to do is armor you so heavily that no matter what they try to do to you, they can't get through.*

Great, she thought. Now the rock's little techs, human and alien, were probably standing by the airlocks with whatever weapons they'd been able to assemble in the last weeks, just waiting for something to try booming in. All she could do was hope they weren't ready for the Wolf.

The hissing of her circulating air was very loud in the small space of the helmet. Reese could feel sweat gathering under the Wolf's padded harness. The rock's short horizon scrolled below her feet. Attitudinal jets made brief adjustments, kept Reese close to the surface. The Wolf's suit monitors were projected, through her interface stud, in a complex multidimensional weave, bright columns glowing in the optical centers of her brain. She watched the little green indicators, paying little attention as long as they stayed green.

The target rolled over the near horizon in an instant—a silver-bright pattern of solar collectors, transmission aerials, dishes pointed at different parts of the sky. In the middle squatted the gleaming bulk of the freighter that had been sent to retrieve the base personnel, its docking tube still connected to the big cargo airlock.

Reese had a number of choices for gaining entry: there were two personnel airlocks, or she could go through one of the freighter locks and then through the docking tube. There were nine personnel on station, five humans and four Powers.

They can brew explosives with the stuff they've got on station, Berger had told her. *But they can't put anything too big around the airlock, or they'd decompress the whole habitat—and they don't have enough stored air to repressurize. They can't set off anything too big inside, or they'd wreck their work. It's too small a place for them to plan anything major. We figure they'll depend on small explosives, and maybe gas.*

The base rolled closer. Reese felt her limbs moving easily in the webbing, the hum of awareness in her nerves and blood. A concrete certainty of her capabilities. All the things she had been unable to live without.

Coolant flow had increased, the suit baking in the sun. The webbing around her body was chafing her.

She thought of explosive, of gas, the way the poison clouds had drifted through the tunnels on Archangel, contaminating everything, forcing her to live inside her suit for days, not even able to take a shit without risking burns on her ass. At least this was going to be quick, however it went.

Reese decided to go in through one of the small personnel airlocks—the brains inside the rock might have decided the cargo ship was expendable and packed its joints with homemade explosive. She maneuvered the Wolf in a slow somersault and dropped feet-first onto the velcro strip by Airlock Two.

Berger wanted her to get in without decompressing the place if she could—there was stuff inside he didn't want messed up. Reese bent and punched the emergency entrance button, and to her surprise she began to feel a faint humming through her feet and the hatch began to roll up. She'd planned to open the hatch manually.

How naive were these people? she wondered. Or was there some surprise in the airlock, waiting for her?

You're gonna c-carry that stuff? Vickers had asked in surprise, as he noticed the pistol snugged under the armpit and the long knife strapped to her leg.

I don't want to depend entirely on the Wolf, she'd said. *If it gets immobilized somehow, I want to be able to surprise whoever did it.*

There'd been an amused grin on Vickers' face. *They immobilize the Wolf, they sure as hell can immobilize you.*

Adjust the webbing anyway, she'd said. Because battle machinery always went wrong sooner or later, because if the mission directive didn't give her backup, she'd just have to be her own. Because she just didn't *like* the Wolf, its streamlined design, its purposeful intent. Because even to someone accustomed to violence, the thing was obscene.

Reese knelt by the airlock, pulled a videocamera from her belt, and held it over the airlock, scanning down and fought back a wave of bile surging into her throat, because the lock was full of dead men.

Mental indicators shifted as, with a push of her mind, she ordered her attitudinal jets to separate the Wolf from the velcro parking strip, then drop into the lock. The dead swam in slow motion as she dropped among them. Her heart crashed in her chest.

The crew of the freighter, she thought. The rebels had put them in here, not having anyplace else. Their skins were gray, the tongues protruding and black. *Some kind of poison.*

"Welcome to Cuervo Gold," she said, and laughed. Nerves.

She hit the button to cycle the airlock, found it refused to work. Incurious dead eyes gazed at her as she cranked the outer door shut manually, then planted thermocharges on the inner door locks. She drifted up to the top of the airlock again, the Wolf's horns scratching the outer door. The dead men rose with her, bumping gently against the Wolf's arms and legs.

Reese curled her legs under her, protecting the Wolf's more vulnerable head and back. Adrenaline was beating a long tattoo in her pulse.

A vulture smile crossed her face. Her nerves sang a mad little song. *Here's where I take it up the ass,* she thought, and pulsed through her wetware the radio code to set off the detonators.

The lock filled with scorching bright light, smoke, molten blobs of bright metal. Air entered the lock with a prolonged scream. Suddenly her olfactory sensors were overwhelmed with the smell of scorched metal, burning flesh. Her gorge rose. She pulsed a command to cut out the smell, then moved down to the inner lock door, seized it, rolled it up with the enhanced strength of the Wolf.

An explosion went off right in her face. Projectiles thudded into corpse flesh, cracked against the faceplate. She and the dead men went flying back, slamming against the outer hatch. Her pulse roared in her ears. She gave the Wolf a command to move down, and move down fast.

Her nerves were shrieking as she smashed into a wall of the airlock, corrected, flew down again, out the lock this time, cracked into another wall. Her teeth rattled. A homemade claymore, she thought, explosive packed in a tube with shrapnel, bits of jagged alloy, wire, junk. Command-detonated, most likely, so that meant someone was here watching the airlock door. Targeting displays flashed bright red on the interior of her faceplate. She turned and fired. Slammed into a wall again. Fired a second time.

The targets died. Fixed to each of the Wolf's upper forearms was a semiautomatic ten-gauge shotgun firing shells packed with poison flechettes. Reese had more deadly equipment available—a small grenade launcher on the left lower forearm, and a submachine gun on the right, gas projectors on her chest—but the op plan was to kill the targets without taking a chance on disturbing any of the valuable equipment or experiments.

Dollops of blood streamed into the near-weightlessness, turning into crimson spheres. A man and a woman, the latter holding some kind of homemade beam weapon she hadn't got the chance to fire, were slowly flying backward toward the sprayed gray plastic walls, their hearts and lungs punctured by a dozen flechettes each. Their faces were frozen in slow-gathering horror at the sight of the Wolf. Reese tried to move, then hit the wall again. She realized the shrapnel had jammed one of her maneuvering jets full on. Her wetware wove routines to compensate, then she leaped past the dying pair and through an open doorway.

No one was in the next series of partitioned rooms, the crew quarters. These people were incredibly naive, she thought, hiding out next to an airlock they knew was going to be blown and not even getting into vac suits. They should have put the claymore on the interior hatch door, not inside the station itself.

Maybe they couldn't face going into where they'd put the crew they'd killed. These weren't professionals, they were a bunch of eggheads who hadn't known what they were getting into when they signed their declaration of independence from a policorp that could not even afford to acknowledge their existence.

They weren't soldiers, but they were still volunteers. They'd already killed people, quite coldly it seemed, in the name of whatever science they were doing here. She clenched her teeth and thought about how some people, no matter how smart they were, remained just too stupid to live.

There was a new bulkhead door welded to the exterior of the crew quarters. Reese blew it open the same way as the airlock, then jetted through. Shrieks sounded on her audio thread, the strange organ sounds Powers made through their upper set of nostrils. Even as her mind squalled at the unearthly sight of a fast-moving, centauroid pair of aliens, she fired. They died before they could fire their home-made weapons. Her mind flashed on the video, the actor-Steward eradicating aliens with his shotgun. An idiotic memory.

She went through a door marked with biohazard warnings. The door gave a soft hiss as she opened it.

The next room was brightly lit, humming with a powerful air conditioning unit, filled with computer consoles plugged into walls of bare metal, not plastic. Cable stretched to and from something that looked like a hundred-liter aquarium filled with what appeared to be living flesh. Strange, she thought. It looked as if the meat were divided by partitions, like honeycomb in a cultured hive. Silver-gray wires, apparently variable-lattice thread, were woven through the meat. Elsewhere an engine hummed as it pumped crimson fluid. Monitors drew jagged lines across screens, holographic digits floated in air.

Weird, she thought again. Alien biochemistry.

There were three other rooms identical to the last. No one was in the first two.

In the third was a single man, gaunt, silver-haired. He was float-ing by the room's aquarium, a frown on his face. He was in a vac suit with the helmet in his hand, giving the impression he simply didn't want to bother to put it on.

He looked at Reese as she came in. There was no fear in his eyes, only sadness.

He spoke as he pushed off from the aquarium, floating to the empty alloy ceiling, where Reese's shot wouldn't hit his experiment by mistake.

"It's over," he said. "Not that it matters."

Reese thought of Steward in the hospital bed, dying for something else equally stupid, equally futile, and filled the man's face with poison darts.

Past the next seal two Powers tried to burn her with acid. The stuff smoked pointlessly on her ceramic armor while she killed them. One of the remaining humans tried to surrender, and the other tried to hide in a toilet. Neither tactic worked. She searched the place thoroughly, found no one else, and disarmed the traps at each of the airlocks.

There was a pain deep in her skull. The air in the suit had begun to taste bad, full of sour sweat, burnt adrenaline. Sadness drifted through her at the waste, the stupidity of it all. Twelve more dead, and all for nothing.

Reese left the bodies where they lay—nobody was paying her to clean the place up—and used the other personnel lock to return to *Voidrunner*. Once she was in sight of the ship she pointed one of her microwave antennae at the ship and gave the code signaling success: "Transmit the following to base. *Mandate. Liquid. Consolidation.*" A combination of words unlikely to be uttered by accident.

She cycled through the ship's central airlock. Pain hammered in her brain, her spine. Time to get out of this obscene contraption. The door opened.

Targeting displays flashed scarlet on the interior of her faceplate. Reese's nerves screamed as the Wolf's right arm, with her arm in it, rose: The ten-gauge exploded twice and the impact spun Vickers back against the opposite wall. He impacted and bounced lightly, already dead. "*No!*" Reese cried, and the Wolf moved forward, brushing the body aside. Reese's arms, trapped in the suit's webbing, rose to a combat stance. She tried to tug them free. Targeting displays were still flashing. Reese tried to take command of the suit through the interface stud. It wouldn't respond.

"Take cover!" Reese shouted. "The Wolf's gone rogue!" She didn't know whether the suit was still on transmit or whether anyone was listening. The Wolf had visible light and IR detectors, motion scanners, scent detectors, sensors that could detect the minute compression wave of a body moving through air.

There was no way the Wolf would miss anyone in the ship, given enough time.

Reese's heart thundered in her chest. "Get into vac suits!" she ordered. "Abandon ship! Get onto the station. Try and hold out there."

Chung's voice snapped over the outside speakers. "Where the hell are you?" At least someone was listening.

"I'm moving upship toward the control room. Oh, fuck." The heads-up display indicated the Wolf had detected motion from the docking cockpit, which meant the armored bulkhead door was open.

The Wolf caught Falkland as he was trying to fly out of the cockpit and get to an airlock. The flechettes failed to penetrate the exoskeleton, so the Wolf flew after him, caught him bodily. Reese felt her left hand curling around the back of Falkland's head, the right hand draw back to strike. She fought against it. Falkland was screaming, trying to struggle out of the Wolf's grip. "*I'm not doing this!*" Reese cried, wanting him to know that, and closed her eyes.

Her right arm punched out once, twice, three times. The Wolf began to move again. When Reese opened her eyes there was blood and bone spattering the faceplate.

"I'm still heading upship," Reese said. "I don't think the Wolf knows where you are."

Chung didn't answer. No point, Reese thought, in his sending a radio signal that might give away his position. The Wolf reached the forward control room, then began a systematic search of the ship, moving aft. Reese reported the suit's movements, hoping to hell he'd get away. The ship was small, and a search wouldn't take long.

Custom thread, Vickers had told her. *Woven into the target acquisition unit.* Berger had done it, she knew, not only wanting to wipe out the station personnel but anyone who knew of Cuervo's existence.

She was riding in an extermination cyberdrone now, trapped inside its obscene, purposeful body.

Mandate. Liquid. Consolidation. The code had sent the Wolf on its rampage. The liquidation is mandated. Consolidate knowledge about Cuervo.

Displays flickered on the screen. The thing had scented Chung. Reese could do nothing but tell him it was coming.

Chung was by the aft airlock, halfway into the rad suit he'd need to flee through the airless engine space.

His face was fixed in an expression of rage. "*Steward!*" Reese screamed. The ten-gauge barked twice, and then the Wolf froze. The displays were gone. The Wolf, still with considerable momentum, continued to drift toward the aft bulkhead. It struck and rebounded, moving slowly toward Chung.

Reese tried to move in the suit, but its joints were locked. Her crashing pulse was the loudest sound in the helmet. She licked sweat from her upper lip, felt it running down her brows. Chung's body slowly collapsed in the insignificant gravity of the asteroid. Drops of blood fell like slow-motion rubies. The gravity wasn't enough to break the surface tension, and the droplets rested on the deck like ball bearings, rolling in the circulating air.

Reese's heart stopped as she realized that the sound of the Wolf's air-circulation system had ceased. She had only the air in the suit, then nothing.

Her mind flailed in panic. Shouting, her cries loud in her ears, she tried to move against the locked joints of the Wolf. The Wolf only drifted slowly to the deck, its limbs immobile.

Like Archangel, she thought. Nothing to look forward to but dying in a suit, in a tunnel, in the smell of your own fear. Just like her officers had always wanted. She tasted bile and fought it down.

I'm using air, she thought, and clamped down, gulping twice, trying to control her jackhammer heart, her panicked breath.

Chung's furious eyes glared into hers at a distance of about three feet. She could see a reflection of the Wolf in his metal teeth. Reese began to move her arms and legs, testing the tension of the web.

There was a pistol under her left arm. If she could get to it with her right hand, she might be able to shoot her way out of the suit somehow.

Fat chance.

But still it was something to do, anyway. She began to move her right arm against the webbing, pulling it back. Blood rubies danced before her eyes. She managed to get her hand out of the glove, but there was a restraining strap against the back of her elbow that prevented further movement. She pushed forward, keeping her hand out of the glove, then drew back. Worked at it slowly, synchronizing the movement with her breath, exhaling to make herself smaller. Steward, she thought, would have been quoting Zen aphorisms to himself. Hers were more direct. *You can get smaller if you want to*, she thought, *you've done it before.*

She got free of the elbow strap, drew her arm back, felt her elbow encounter the wall of the suit. She was beginning to pant. The air can't be gone this quickly, she thought, and tried to control panic as she pulled back on her arm, as pain scraped along her nerves. Sweat was coating her body. She tried to think herself smaller. She could feel warm blood running down her arm. The Wolf was saturated with the scent of fear.

Reese screamed as her arm came free, part agony, part exultation. She reached across her chest, felt the butt of the pistol. It was cold in her hand, almost weightless.

Where to point it? She could try blowing out the faceplate, but she'd have the barrel within inches of her face, and the faceplate was damn near impervious anyway. The bullet would probably ricochet right into her head. The Wolf was too well armored. Chung's angry glare was making it impossible for her to think. Reese closed her eyes and tried to think of the schematics she'd studied, the location of the variable-lattice thread that contained the suit's instructions.

Behind her, she thought. Pressed against her lower spine was the logic thread that operated the Wolf's massive limbs. If she could wreck the thread, the locked limbs might move.

She experimented with the pistol. There wasn't enough room to completely angle the gun around her body.

Sweat floated in salty globes around her as she thought it through, tried desperately to come up with another course of action. The air grew foul. Reese decided that shooting herself with the pistol would be quicker than dying of asphyxiation.

She tried to crowd as far over to the right as possible, curling the gun against her body, holding it reversed with her thumb on the trigger. The cool muzzle pressed into her side, just below the ribs. *Line it up carefully*, she thought. *You don't want to have to do this more than once.* She tried to remember anatomy and what was likely to get hit. A kidney? Adrenal glands?

Here's where I really take it up the ass, she thought. She screamed, building rage, and fired... and then screamed again from pain. Sweat bounced against the faceplate, spattering in the fierce momentum of the bullet's pressure wave.

The Wolf's limbs unlocked and the cyberdrone sagged to the deck. Reese gave a weak cheer, then shrieked again from the pain.

She had heard it wasn't supposed to hurt when you got hit, not right away. Another lie, she thought, invented by the officer class.

There was something wrong with the world, with the way it was manifesting itself. She realized she was deaf from the pistol blast.

Reese leaned back, took a deep breath of foul air. Now, she thought, comes the easy part.

Reese managed to put her right arm back into the sleeve, then use both arms—the armor, thankfully, was near weightless—to get herself out of the suit. She moved to the sick bay and jabbed endorphin-analogue into her thigh, then X-rayed herself on the portable machine. It looked as if she hadn't hit anything vital, but then she wasn't practiced at reading X-rays, either. She patched herself up, swallowed antibiotics, and then out of nowhere the pain slammed down, right through the endorphin. Every muscle in her body went into spasm. Reese curled into a ball, her body a flaming agony. She bounced gently off one wall, then another. Fought shuddering waves of nausea. Tears poured from her eyes. It hurt too much to scream.

It went on forever, for days. Loaded on endorphins, she looted the station, moving everything she could into the freighter, then pissed bright blood while howling in agony. Fevers raged in her body. She filled herself with antibiotics and went on working. Things—people, aliens, hallucinations—kept reaching at her, moving just outside her field of vision. Sometimes she could hear them talking to her in some strange, melodic tongue.

She grappled *Voidrunner* to the freighter's back, then lifted off Cuervo and triggered the charges. She laughed at the bright blossoms of flame in the locks, the gush of air that turned to white snow in the cold vacuum, and then into a bright rainbow as it was struck by the sun. Reese accelerated toward Earth for as long as she could stand it, then cut the engines.

There was a constant wailing in her ears, the cry of the fever in her blood. For the next several days—one of them was her birthday— Reese hung weightless in her rack, fought pain and an endless hot fever, and studied the data she'd stolen, trying to figure out why nine tame scientists were willing to commit murder over it.

The fever broke, finally, under the onslaught of antibiotics. Her urine had old black blood now, not bright new crimson. She thought she was beginning to figure out what the station crew had been up to.

It was time to decide where she was going to hide. The freighter and the tug were not registered to her, and her appearance with them was going to result in awkward questions. She thought about forging records of a sale—credentials, after all, were her specialty. Reese decided to tune in on the broadcasts from Earth and see if there were any new places for refugees to run to.

To her surprise she discovered that Ram's executive board on Prince Station had fallen three days before, and Cheney had been made the new chairman. She waited another two days, studying the data she'd stolen, the bottles of strange enzymes and tailored RNA she had moved to the freighter's cooler, and then beamed a call to Prince and asked for S. C. Vivekenanda. She was told the vice president of communications was busy. "I can wait," she said. "Tell him it's Waldman."

Ken's voice came on almost immediately. "Where are you?" he asked.

"I'm coming your way," Reese told him. "And I think I've got your architecture of liberation with me. But first, we've got to cut a deal."

What the lab's inhabitants had been up to wasn't quite what Ken had been talking about that gusty spring night in Uzbekistan, but it was close. The Brighter Suns biologists and artificial intelligence people had been working on a new way of storing data, a fast and efficient way, faster than variable-lattice thread.

They had succeeded in storing information in human DNA.

It had been tried before. Genetically altered humanity had been present for a century, and the mysteries of the genetic mechanism had been thoroughly mapped. There had long been theories that genetic material, which succeeded in coding far more information on its tiny strand than any comparable thread-based technology, would provide the answer to the endless demand for faster and more efficient means of data storage.

The theories had always failed when put into practice. Just because specialists could insert desirable traits in a strand of human DNA didn't mean they had the capability of doing it at the speed of light, reading the genetic message the strand contained at similar speed, or altering the message at will. The interactions of ribosomes, transfer RNA, and enzymes were complex and interrelated to the point where the artificial intelligence/biologist types had despaired of trying to control them with current technology.

Alien genetics, it turned out, were simple compared to the human. Power DNA chains were much shorter, containing half the two hundred thousand genes in a human strand, without the thousands of repetitions and redundancies that filled human genes. Their means of reproducing DNA were similar, but similarly streamlined.

And the Power method of DNA reproduction was compatible with human genetics. The transfer and message RNA were faster, cleaner, more controllable. Information transfer had a theoretically astounding speed—a human DNA strand, undergoing replication, unwound at 8000 RPM. Power RNA combined with human DNA made data transfers on thread look like slow motion.

Once the control technology was developed, information could be targeted to specific areas of the DNA strand. The dominant genes could remain untouched; but the recessive genes could be altered to contain information. Nothing could be kept secret when any spy could code information in his own living genetic makeup. And no one could discover the spy unless they knew what code he was using and what they were looking for.

The architecture of liberation. Risk-free transfer of data. It would be years before any of this was possible—Prince Station's newly hired biologists would have to reconstruct all the station's work and then develop it to the point where it was commercially viable. But Prince Station was going to have its new source of technology, and Reese a new source of income—she'd asked for a large down payment in advance of a small royalty that should nevertheless make her a billionaire in the next forty years. She'd asked for that, plus Prince's help in disposing of a few other problems.

Reese looked down at her double, lying on a bed in a room that smelled of death. Her twin's eyes were closed, her breasts rose and fell under a pale blue sheet. Bile rose in Reese's throat.

Reese was blond again, her nose a little straighter, her mouth a little wider. She had a new kidney, a new eardrum. New fingerprints, new blue irises. She liked the new look. The double looked good, too.

Two bodies, a man and a woman, were sprawled at the foot of the bed: assassins, sent by Berger to kill her. They had followed a carefully laid trail to her location here on Prince, and when they came into her apartment they'd been shot dead by Prince's security men firing from concealment in the wide bedroom closet. Reese had waited safely in the next room, her nerves burning with adrenaline fire while she clutched Ken's hand; her nerves alert for the sound of gunfire, she watched her double breathe under its sheet.

Then the security people came for the mannikin. They were going to kill it.

The double was Reese's clone. Her face had been restructured the same way Reese's had, and her artificial eyes were blue. Her muscles had been exercised via electrode until they were as firm as Reese's. There was even a metal pin in her ankle, a double of the one Reese carried. The clone was an idiot—her brain had never contained Reese's mind.

The idea was to make it appear that Reese and the assassins had killed each other. Reese looked down at her double and felt her mouth go dry. The security people were paddling around the room, trying to make appearances perfect. Hot anger blazed behind Reese's eyes. *Fuck this*, she thought.

She pried the pistol out of one of the assassins' hands and raised it.

She was a tunnel rat, she thought. An animal, a coward, disloyal. Sometimes she needed reminding.

"It's not murder," Ken said, trying to help.

"Yes it is," Reese said. She raised the killer's gun—an ideal assassin's weapon, a compressed-air fletcher—and fired a silent dart into the mannikin's thigh. Then she closed her eyes, not wanting to see the dying thing's last spasm. Instead she saw Steward, dying in his own silent bed, and felt a long gray wave of sadness. She opened her eyes and looked at Ken.

"It's also survival," she said.

"Yes. It is."

A cold tremor passed through Reese's body. "I wasn't talking about the clone."

While Ken's assistants made it look as if she and the assassins had killed each other, Reese stepped through the hidden door into the next apartment. Her bag was already packed, her identity and passport ready. Credentials, she thought, her specialty. That and killing helpless people. Group rates available.

She wanted to live by water again. New Zealand sounded right. It was getting to be spring there now.

"You'll come back?" Ken asked.

"Maybe. But in the meantime, you'll know where to send the royalties." There was pain in Ken's eyes, in Steward's eyes. Attachments were weakness, always a danger. Reese had a vision of the Street, people parting, meeting, dying, in silence, alone. She wouldn't be safe on Prince and couldn't be a part of Ken's revolution. She was afraid she knew what it was going to turn into, once it became the sole possessor of a radical new technology. And what that would turn Ken into.

Reese shouldered her bag. Her hands were still trembling. Sadness beat slowly in her veins. She was thirty-seven now, she thought. Maybe there were sports she shouldn't indulge in.

Maybe she should just leave.

"Enjoy your new architecture," she said, and took off.

The Defense of Gipper's Twist

NATHAN W. TORONTO

Nathan W. Toronto taught military operations and strategy to military officers for ten years before becoming a management consultant in Washington, DC. This story is a future warfare retelling of the tactical morality play, *The Defence of Duffer's Drift*, by Ernest Swinton. "The Defense of Gipper's Twist" was a finalist in the 2017 U.S. Army TRADOC Science Fiction Writing Contest.

JUNGLE HUMIDITY IS MURDER for Army-issued HUDs. Mine stopped working about 24.38 seconds after we touched down at Tocumen Airport, so I switched on my aftermarket specs and connected them by laser cable to the STAC—Systemic Tactical Awareness Controller. My old man gave me the specs as a graduation gift (West Point class of 2048). How he knew my Army-issued gear would stop working so quickly, I can't say.

I stowed my HUD and shrugged at Staff Sergeant Morris. "Figures. Aftermarket tech works better."

Morris grunted and motioned for the other human members of the HST (hybrid strike team) to debark. Morris had been distant the whole flight.

"Sergeant Morris," I said, pulling my ruck onto my shoulder. "I hope this doesn't feel like a babysitting assignment."

His eyes narrowed. "It's not that, sir. We didn't even rate a C-17 from Bragg, and we didn't even get to jump from the plane. Panama's been quiet for twenty years, and we have ROEs so strict they wired them into the STAC." He flipped down his HUD and STACked in, nodding towards the rear ramp in frustration. "Besides, a whole HST is overkill for a three-day area defense mission."

We were to secure the Ronald W. Reagan Omnidirectional Space Elevator Transition Station—Gipper's Twist, for short—the start point for one of four feeder cables to the main cable, anchored somewhere in the Caribbean. Gipper's Twist, connected to the Port of Gamboa by a 15K rail line, was the first link between a major seaport and Midway Station, a spaceport tethered in mid-earth orbit. Someday the elevator would extend to geostationary orbit, but for now we had to keep things calm on the ground so SECDEF could cut the ribbon at Gipper's Twist, in three days.

Back at Bragg, my CO had grinned. "What a great assignment for you, LT! We'll show the Ruskis and the Chinese that our elevator is better than theirs."

With a slap on the back he told me how hooah I was and stuffed my team and me, along with our gear, into the cabin of a rickety C-130. The carbon fiber skin and EM (electromagnetic) drive turbofan engines were a new lease on life for the old airframe, but after nine decades in production even Hercules starts to wear down.

I stepped from the ramp and wiped my brow as Morris strode toward the three Panamanian vehicles idling on the tarmac. He looked back at me and made a face. "And we have to ride in rusty old MRAPs."

I ignored him and blinked into my specs to check progress. Drones were already in, and they were almost done with the rattle tubes (rapid-firing, self-propelled mortar tubes with STAC-targeting and turbo-cooling systems). The MECHs (Military Engineering and Combat Hybrids) would go last, since we'd use them when we got to Gipper's Twist to establish a wide area perimeter. No sense in defending Gipper's Twist by just sitting on it. I mean, who hasn't read *The Defence of Duffer's Drift*?

Morris commed over the STAC. "Ready, sir."

I climbed into my MRAP, brimming with anticipation.

The terrain around Gipper's Twist lent itself to the defense. The jungle had been cleared well away from the station to make room for the railway junction and other infrastructure, like warehouses and the road to the village. As soon as defensive preparations were under way, I went to the top of the rise and sketched out the terrain. We had clean lines-of-sight and a lot of options for setting up interlocking fields of fire.

Our thirty MECHs helped set up the defensive strong points. MECHs performed combat engineering tasks, and their heat and IR signatures mimicked a human's. In a firefight, they could shoot, move, and communicate with their human controller over the STAC, so the enemy would have a hard time distinguishing them from human All Domain Soldiers.

The twelve ADSs in our team, including Sergeant Morris and me, covered all warfare domains. We had four ground combat controllers and two each of combat engineer, air domain, fires, and information domain controllers. Most of us could cross-operate in a pinch, and we could all fight the old-fashioned way. You know, duty, honor, country, and all that. The brass hated it, but we called ourselves "addies". "All Domain Soldiers" took too much breath.

With the MECHs, rattle tubes, and drones (fifteen unarmed for surveillance, comms, and targeting and five long-loiter ground attack drones), we had quite the firepower in our team. We also counted on continuous satellite and nextgen Global Hawk all spectrum sur-veillance and targeting, STACked in seamlessly so we could see and shoot everywhere, even when it wasn't line-of-sight. In a real bind, satellite-based high velocity micromissiles, tipped with autotargeting explosive or inertial warheads, could rain death on the enemy. The ROEs were restrictive—no engagement outside the 1000 meter radius from Gipper's Twist, and no concentrated fires—but our team had warfare covered.

Confident, I put the CP in the Gipper's Twist control tower, kept an info addy, an air addy, and two MECHs with me, and assigned the rest of the combat power to strong points on the rise south of the CP, on the rail line leading into the jungle, and in the village, where I put our best marksaddies ("marksmen" is too gender-specific). I doffed my battle rattle and paid a courtesy call to the foreman of the work crew, who had a gentle demeanor and a Russian calendar that looked out of place on his wall. We exchanged pleasantries and he admired my specs, so I let him put them on. I put Morris in charge of organizing recon patrols, and instructed him to buzz my STAC if anything appeared amiss in the night. With a smile, I wiped the sweat from my brow, straightened my mosquito netting, and went to sleep in less time than it took my Army-issued HUD to malfunction.

The buzz of bullets zipping through the CP startled me into consciousness. Brow furrowed, I reached for my helmet and weapon, then checked whether I was STACked in. I blinked into my specs. Nothing.

"Sergeant Morris, do you copy?"

Nothing.

The two addies in the CP jumped out of their cots and activated the MECHs, then took defensive positions. I blinked into my specs again, but the battlefield overlay menu didn't activate. All I saw were grenade bursts and muzzle flashes in the night.

"Burns and Gill, whaddya got?"

"STAC's down, sir," said Burns, the info addy, with powerful understatement.

Gill, the air addy, tapped his HUD. "Sir, we don't have STAC targeting or spectrum overlay, but we do have visibility for team air assets. We can..."

Thwuck! A bullet zinged through the window and hit Gill in the face. He slumped over, and instinct kicked in.

"MECH, cover my zone! Burns, help me."

Burns and I tried to staunch the blood, to revive him, but we failed. Bullets kept whizzing through the CP. Panic rose in my chest. Cut off from my team. I'd lost a man.

I stumbled over to my position, head spinning, the image of Gill's still body seared onto my mind. Yet another volley of bullets zipped through the CP, and my mind sprang to clarity. I rummaged through my ruck, hands crusty, and fished out my radio. I clenched my jaw and clipped the radio onto my shoulder harness, then returned fire.

I craned my head down to open the radio channel with my cheek. "Morris?"

"Sir, was your radio off? Lost STAC. Troops in contact at all strong points. Lost Jones and fifteen MECHs. Estimate enemy strength fifty fighters. Not clear how they jammed us."

I slammed my fist on the window sill. Two addies down. "What do you need, Sergeant?"

"Sir, rattle tubes are offline. Can you get us fires?"

"All the fires you want." Screw the ROEs. "You laze 'em. I'll blaze 'em."

When the enemy popped up, we smashed him, courtesy of my team's lasers and our ground attack drones. Problem was, the explosives twisted up the rail line and flattened one of the warehouses. The twisted metal and rubble were too much to clean up in two days. After the shooting stopped, I realized that the legal mess my concentrated fires created would take even longer than that to clean up. SECDEF couldn't come down like this.

My CO told me to hold a presser for local media to explain why the ribbon-cutting ceremony would be delayed.

Before the presser Burns came over to me, somber. "Sir, ran some STAC diagnostics. We had a hack. Your aftermarket specs."

I took off my specs and examined them with a wary eye. A dull metallic bead, about the size of a tick, was attached to the interior of the left temple. Then I remembered the foreman I showed them to, the one with the Russian calendar hanging on the wall.

I groaned, then considered the lessons learned:

- Controlling information systems won't ensure victory, but you're not going to win if you let the enemy hack you.

- When precision targeting breaks down, mass and firepower are still measured in effect, sometimes with strategic consequences.

- Battlefield terrain is composed of geography and information. And humans.

I woke to the gentle hum of four EM drive turbofan engines. I didn't stop to think about whether yesterday was a dream, but applied the lessons, glad for a chance at redemption.

I tapped Sergeant Morris' shoulder and plugged into the C-130's comm system, signaling channel two.

"Sergeant Morris, STAC check, then test line-of-sight comms."

"Roger, sir. I'll start Burns on a full STAC diagnostic," he said, reaching for his LOS comm card and holding it up for the team to see.

While the team rummaged for their own cards, I continued my instructions. "Launch drone patrols from the aircraft so we can have all spectrum recon as soon as we hit the ground, even beyond the ROE perimeter. We need a clear picture of the human and information terrain."

Morris nodded, then motioned for the team to STAC in. I flipped down my HUD to monitor the STAC check. When my HUD started wigging, I passed it to Burns.

By the time I climbed into the ancient MRAP, I boasted a functional, Army-issued HUD, complete with active cyber diagnostics.

On route to Gipper's Twist, air recon gave us a baseline information and human terrain picture. The density of human activity around the station surprised me, mostly construction workers going back and forth, but the information picture blew me away. The village was thick with signals, centered on the foreman's house.

This time, I trudged over there with Burns, and I kept my gear on. Before rapping on the door, I nodded to Burns. He circled around the house to find the source of the flow.

The foreman answered, fat fingers holding the doorknob. "*Hola*, you must be security. *Bienvenidos*."

His demeanor brimmed with levity, but I couldn't trust my mission to this man's geniality. All the same, I couldn't alienate him three days before the work was complete, so I yanked off my glove, flipped on my realtime digital interpreter and stuck out my hand. "Pleasure, sir."

Entering his house for the second time, the same unremarkable interior met my eyes as before. I checked for clues that might explain the information flow. A decrepit plasma screen hung on the wall and a dusty cell phone made a home on the mantel, but there was nothing to suggest the place had left the twentieth century. I blinked into the STAC and messaged Burns: Cut the line.

The house buzzed with rapid-fire Spanish, too fast for my digital interpreter to pick up. The foreman's eyes darted this way and that. He shrugged in mock apology and shuffled out of the room.

A young woman emerged from the back, wiping wet hands on her bright pink apron, wearing a smile to match. "My father asks if you will please come back later."

I raised an eyebrow with as much nonchalance as I could muster and held up a hand. "No problem. Could you tell him that I'd like to gather the workers after the evening meal? I want to offer some words of encouragement."

"*Sí.*" She smiled and eyed the door with a please-leave-now look.

I pinged Morris as soon as my boot hit dirt. "You know the card security system for the construction workers?"

"Yes, sir."

"Have handheld scanners ready to check worker IDs. I've invited them for a pep talk after chow tonight."

"Roger. I'll detail some MECHs for crowd control, and we'll check cards against the worker manifest."

I smiled and blinked to ping Gill.

"Sir?" Gill said.

"Focus extra air assets on the village, and get the sat link up. I want to know if there are any suspicious comings and goings tonight, especially after we check IDs."

"Wilco, sir."

With our strong points set, and with the all spectrum overlay streaming through my HUD, I felt confident that we had secured Gipper's Twist for the night. All the workers on the manifest came and had their cards checked after chow, and I blathered on about the future, pan-American brotherhood, and the riches the cable would bring. A couple of workers came up, exchanged nervous glances and said something about "other workers", but my interpreter didn't follow the dialect. They walked off.

We were ready, though. At 2300, the patrols set, I laid down on my cot in the CP, giving strict instructions for Gill and Burns to wake me at the first sign of trouble.

I woke to a thunderous boom and the STAC alert buzzing in my ear. The CP shook. I bolted upright and reached for my weapon, half expecting to feel the tower topple underneath us. I slapped on my helmet and HUD, then worked my way out of the mosquito netting.

Burns and Gill were already up. I STACked in and scrolled through the battlefield overlays. Explosion at Warehouse 1. Small arms fire north and east of the village.

"Burns and Gill, give me an air and info picture."

"Sir," said Gill, "targeting and recon for air assets are glitchy. We can find, but not fix and destroy."

Gill: "Enemy is using handheld jammers with frequency skipping. Definitely Russian tech, sir."

Morris' air controller STACked through with a fire mission. The battle map on my HUD showed enemy fighters engaging from just outside the ROE perimeter. Occasionally they'd come inside, but not long enough for the rattle tubes to engage with precision, at least not without massing fires.

I scratched my chin. "Gill, patch into the sat and get some inertial micros on their way from low-earth orbit." The jammers wouldn't work as well on the slim-profile missiles, and they auto-targeted the last thousand feet of descent.

Another explosion went off by the rail line. The STAC's alarm buzzed again, and I blinked it off to reveal a third squad-size element attacking us. I blinked through the overlays. We didn't have any addy casualties, but total enemy strength was over fifty. The LEO sat only had forty missiles allocated to our team, and we were supposed to assume fifty percent targeting accuracy.

"Gill, how long before we have targeting back?"

"Sir, by triangulating drone, Global Hawk, and sat data, I can code a way around enemy jamming. Three minutes, sir."

"Roger," I said. "When that's up, use rattle tubes to funnel the enemy inside the ROE perimeter. Then we can target with small arms."

"Wilco, sir."

I followed the engagement on my HUD. A group of fighters funneled into the perimeter, but hugged the warehouse just before LEO missile impact, so only three of the fifteen went down. Other groups went to ground outside the perimeter, then disappeared from the STAC.

I pulled up the all spectrum imaging overlay, but the enemy fighters were gone. "Gill," I said, "confirm contact lost with hostile force to the north."

Pregnant pause. "Sir, confirmed."

An eerie silence settled. Didn't feel right. I pursed my lips. We knew where they were, and in what numbers, but had no idea what they intended.

I pinged Jones, a fires controller at the rail line strong point, and asked for a SITREP.

"Sir," she said, "they shot our MECHs all up, but didn't even target us. Had real good aim, sir."

Before I had time to process how our air and space surveillance capability could have lost track of two dozen enemy fighters, or how they targeted our MECHs, an explosion rang out from the direction of the warehouses, followed by the pucker of small arms fire.

"Morris," I commed.

"On it, sir."

A message came over the STAC from one of the village MECHs: "Unarmed civilian running from station. Detain?"

I blinked an affirmative and said, "On route."

By the time I got there the young woman from the foreman's house lay tazed and shaking on the ground. A two-foot pipe lay nearby. I leaned down to check her pulse and turned to the MECH. "Was that really necessary?"

"She struck me with that pipe." The MECH then produced a dusty old cell phone, just like the one I'd seen on the foreman's mantel. I raised an eyebrow. "Summarize contents, MECH."

Videos of workers wounded by rattle tube fire and members of my team aiming rifles at figures fleeing into the jungle appeared on my HUD, along with GIFs posted to social media. Hashtags like #AmericanImperialism and #UnsafeCable made the intent plain.

Her eyes flickered open. She sat up and gave me a surly glare. Off towards the warehouses, the engagement died off, and the pregnant silence returned. While the young woman fumed, another attack began back at the rail line. The sun had cleared the treeline, and the young woman's knowing glance told me they had accomplished everything they set out to do, and I had not.

With a grimace, I turned on my heel and strode back to the CP, thinking of ways to explain to my CO how things had gotten so out of hand. Of course, he told me to hold a local presser. As I composed my opening statement, I considered the lessons learned:

- Space may be the ultimate high ground, but it holds little advantage without understanding the human terrain.

- Information is like water; you can influence its currents, but you can't control its content.

- Modern war is a race against time, a deadly game of hide-and-seek where no one knows who's "it". With precision targeting and microfirepower, whoever gets found first loses.

- A clear picture of the enemy disposition is no substitute for understanding his intent.

I awoke once again to the welcome sound of turbofan engines humming through the carbon-fiber fuselage of a well-aged C-130. I gave Sergeant Morris the same instructions as before, with the addition that Burns should insinuate zero-day malware on all networks in the vicinity of Gipper's Twist, just in case. I ordered Morris to create a quick reaction force, and Jones to lead patrols through the jungle, outside the ROE perimeter, to lay passive sensors.

When we got to the foreman's house, instead of cutting the network line and revealing our intent, I instead had Burns splice in, both to install his malware and to feed information back to the States, in case anyone in the village was part of known networks. I asked the foreman to demonstrate the station's capabilities for me, and I had Gill take high-resolution video of a shipping container ascending into the sky. The container was empty, and we brought it back down after a thousand feet, but the video that Gill produced would help steer the narrative about Gipper's Twist on social media. The video went viral, so I had Gill follow me around for the rest of the evening, inspecting construction progress, addressing the workers, and offering a substantial CERP bonus to the whole crew if they finished the project a day early.

The video fun stopped at night, though. "Sergeant Morris," I said over the STAC, "enforce a nighttime curfew. Have Burns set up a thorough permit investigation process should anyone decide they want to leave their homes anyway."

"Wilco, sir."

I didn't even bother with a CP, much less a cot and mosquito netting. I would not fail this time. I caught some sleep here and there during battlefield circulation. Things were quiet until about 0200, when Gill's voice came over the STAC: "Sir, three groups of four individuals heading into the jungle. Passing drone feed to you now."

I examined the feed. How'd they avoid the curfew patrols? "Looks like they're converging on a point in the jungle," I said. "Jones, can you intercept?"

"Yes, sir. We'll be waiting for them."

"Sergeant Morris," I said. "Have there been any curfew violations?"

"None, sir. Their spectrum signatures appeared all of a sudden in the jungle, but they match signatures we logged in the village earlier. Not sure how they got there."

"Sir," said Gill, "all spectrum imaging indicates a possible weapons cache at Jones' rendezvous point."

"Jones," I said, "if they touch those weapons, detain them, but do not engage with lethal force."

"Wilco, sir," said Jones. "In position now."

I watched the confrontation unfold on my HUD. The twelve villagers converged on the rendezvous point, and Jones' patrol enveloped them with practiced skill, silent. The villagers opened up the cache, and Jones and her patrol pounced.

"Sir," she said. "Eleven men and one woman detained. Gave up without a fight." She paused, but kept the channel open. "Uh, sir, these aren't your average narco weapons. These are high-end AKs with signature diffusion and all spectrum sights. Chinese manufacture. They could pick off MECHs from well inside the jungle without having to worry about hitting a human."

A shiver ran through my spine. They were much better equipped than I thought they would be.

Morris commed. "Sir, a couple of MECHs and I located the spot where one set of signatures popped onto the STAC. Found a late-model handheld tunnel digger. Even has the original manufacturer plate in Cyrillic. They had plenty of time from curfew till now to tunnel into the jungle."

"Good work, Morris and Jones. Jones, bring those villagers and hold them in Warehouse 1. Burns, take two MECHs and begin processing and interrogation. Be ready to launch the zero day if things get hot." I smiled at the battlefield overlay on my HUD, completely devoid of enemy activity, but I wasn't about to get cocky. "Stay alert, Team. This isn't over."

I went to confront the foreman. "Before few days," he said, "men with guns come and threaten my daughter and me. We had to take in those twelve, like they were workers."

He refused to say anything more, so I detained him and his daughter, mostly for their own protection.

A new day dawned, and I let myself believe that we could succeed. The day passed without incident, even without the foreman directing things. Workers scrambled to put the finishing touches on Gipper's Twist: siding the station, seeding grass in the soil, painting parking lot lines, installing electrical fixtures. My team and I watched them carefully. It looked like Gipper's Twist would actually be done a day early, so I contacted Bragg to finalize my CERP request and offered local media a sneak peek of Gipper's Twist, one day before the ribbon-cutting. It would be a real coup: award the crew their bonuses and show local media a container rising into the morning sky.

The next night passed without incident, and I afforded myself the luxury of a cot. I could almost see SECDEF's beaming face as she shook my hand with a firm attaboy. We just needed to pass one more tranquil night, then we would be home free.

I took off my battle rattle for the local media event. I unplugged my STAC and donned soft cover. More approachable and human that way. I stood in the parking lot with a clutch of local media. To the click of cameras and typing thumbs, and using my digital interpreter, I explained how Gipper's Twist would endure as a symbol of pan-American togetherness and prosperity. With a flourish, I motioned towards the shipping container as it entered Gipper's Twist on the rail line, explained how the twist mechanism lifted it from the rail line to the cable, and smiled as the container began rising from the station roof behind me.

But then the cable machinery stopped. I turned, and a pit opened in my stomach. Something snapped and the container fell back into the roof and crashed down inside the station. The concussion blew out the windows. A section of siding fell off the station. My blood went cold as I realized that the cameras and thumbs hadn't stopped.

I called off the demonstration, but the press walked off smiling with glee at America's humiliation. I dreaded the hashtags I'd see that afternoon.

I was already composing contrite words for my report when Burns ran up with my STAC earpiece and HUD. "Sir, Bragg finally got back with that human networks report you requested. Thirty names came up. We got twelve that first night, but eighteen others were in the work crew yesterday."

I took the earpiece from Burns and shoved the laser cable into my HUD. When the systems synched, I switched on my private channel with Sergeant Morris. "SITREP."

"Sir, Gipper's Twist has flexiglass. Even with that container falling in, those windows should've held. A combat engineer checked out the siding, and he thinks some of the workers put microdet behind it. The crashing container disguised the sound of the detonation, which was probably set off remotely."

Sabotage. For maximum media effect. We were so close. After sending my report, I reflected on the lessons learned:

- In an information vacuum every military action is tactical, but as long as communications hold out any action can become strategic. Unfortunately, information vacuums do not exist.

- Achieving information dominance is important, but it's just as important to retain and exploit that dominance.

- Technology enables economy of force and a clear picture of the human terrain, but controlling the human terrain requires material influence.

- Hubris is a fickle friend.

I woke once again and sighed in relief at the forgiving turbofan hum of the C-130's engines. Determined to apply what I learned, I organized the team for maximum effect, as before: drone patrols, quick reaction force, strong points, jungle patrol, zero day malware. I even requested a human networks report on the worker manifest as soon as possible, marking it high priority so I'd get it back within twelve hours instead of two days.

Instead of trying to control events as they occurred, I trusted my team to operate based on mission intent. Every addy had a responsibility, and I rotated around the battlefield to lend support, encourage decisiveness, and empower initiative. Together, Jones and Morris sussed out enemy movements on the first night. Based on the human networks report, Burns waylaid certain individuals with time consuming questions and paperwork. Gill detected messages to Russian contacts in Colombia asking for microdet and drones to activate it. I used the CERT bonuses, but I also gave references to authorities at the Port of Gamboa for any workers who wanted to move away from the influence of narcotraffickers.

And I didn't hold a local presser the day before SECDEF's ribbon-cutting ceremony. I documented progress at Gipper's Twist on social media, but I didn't accept more risk than was necessary.

The night before the ribbon-cutting, I stole a few hours' sleep, then woke at midnight to circulate. The day before had been cooler than normal, and fog descended in the wee hours. At 0335 muzzle flashes and grenade blasts ripped open the pre-dawn.

"STAC in, everyone. Trust your buddy and use your overlays."

Burns launched the zero day, in case any villagers had second thoughts about which was the right side to support. My HUD showed 112 fighters hunkered down outside the ROE perimeter, plunking sniper fire into my team's positions. We had a few MECHs damaged, but we dominated air, space, and information domains, and the enemy didn't target our addies. A real twenty-first century standoff.

Then Jones got hit. Lower extremity. Nothing really dangerous, but it was enough, so I got on the horn to Bragg and asked my CO to approve an expansion of the ROE perimeter.

"The longer this goes on, the worse it'll be for us," I argued.

"Approved," said my CO, "but higher says to employ just enough firepower to get them to withdraw. Nothing more. Airborne."

"All the way, sir."

Our LEO missiles and rattle tubes savaged the enemy as soon as the STAC expanded the ROE perimeter, and at 0407 the enemy started to withdraw. The STAC overlay showed them carrying off about 40 casualties, but we couldn't say if they were dead or wounded.

I led a patrol into the jungle to see what I could find out about the enemy. They didn't leave many clues, aside from some bloody foliage and shell casings, but we took samples anyway. On the way back to the village, I considered how decisive an advantage all-domain dominance is.

Before the ribbon-cutting ceremony the next day, as we waited for SECDEF, Burns leaned over to me. "Sir, the DNA analysis came back on that foliage. Mostly Latin genes, but some Russian as well." He grinned and raised his eyebrows. *"Spetsnaz?"*

I turned up the corners of my mouth. "Don't let it get to your head, Burns."

SECDEF's convoy pulled up outside Gipper's Twist. She got out of her black SUV and strode up to me. "Attaboy, LT Forehand Hindsight," she said, pumping my hand up and down. "You've made America proud."

Uncertainty Principle

> Nathan W. Toronto is a data scientist and scholar of
> civil-military relations. He is the author of *How
> Militaries Learn: Human Capital, Military Education,
> and Battlefield Effectiveness* and *Rise of Ahrik*, a
> military science fiction novel. He is not a pet person,
> but he is wary of cats that walk through walls.

THE DAY IT HAPPENED, kittens were the furthest thing from my mind. The day was so blue-sky, hot-dog-grilling, bird-chirpingly happy that something bad was bound to happen.

For the rest of time, or at least for the few minutes humanity has left, debate will rage over whether it was one or two kittens in the Oval Office that day. But that wasn't the issue. The President told me what he told me. I have no idea how the kitten color-shifted like that, but what'll really eat at me (before life on Earth burns to a crisp) is why the black one had it in for us.

Sure enough, on that beautiful day a Cicassian battle cruiser parked itself in geostationary orbit, and I fielded a frantic call from the National Ops Center.

Cicassians are the nastiest alien species known to man, so it was my job as SECDEF to pass on the news and answer the Whiskey-Tango-Foxtrot question that I knew was swimming in the President's head.

"Mr. President, there's a—"

"There's a kitten in my office, Sam."

"Sir? Uh, there's also a—"

"You know how sometimes a kitten follows you home and then it's yours? Well, this one's looking at me like I followed it home."

I cleared my throat. "There's a Cicassian—"

"Wait, it just changed colors. It was white, and now it's black."

How was I supposed to know that this was the kitten, the one the Cicassian high military command sends down when they want to send a message? Hindsight is twenty-twenty, you know? Instead, I figured the President had lost his marbles.

"Mr. President, I...Forget it."

The President chuckled. "I'll call the white one Shrew, and the black one Digger."

"That's very nice, Sir." Like an idiot, I decided to put our nuclear forces on high alert. I mean, was I supposed to just let them come for us?

Apparently, yes. That was what the message said, wrapped in black-and-white kitten. After the alert, things went downhill pretty quickly. Cicassians never wait to shoot second.

The next day, while the whole world sizzled and social media filled the artificially shortened twenty-two hour news cycle with pictures of missiles and white-hot energy beams raining down, the President called me from Air Force One.

"Sam, I never liked black cats."

"Mr. President, I don't think that matters anymore."

"I fed the white kitten, but not the black one. I took the food away from the black one. It hissed at me."

"I thought it was the same animal, Sir."

"I don't think that matters anymore."

But it did matter. Immensely. If the kitten hadn't turned black when it was hungry, we might all still be alive. Heck, maybe in some alternate universe the kitten stayed white, and now we still grill hot dogs and listen to birds chirp against blue skies.

Barren Moon

MAJOR CRAIG MAYBEE, U.S. ARMY

Craig Maybee is a U.S. Army officer and amateur science fiction writer. "Barren Moon" appeared in the January 2020 issue of *Military Review* and originated as a Master's monograph at the U.S. Army School of Advanced Military Studies. The Army turns to graduates of SAMS—SAMSters, as they're called—to solve all of its hardest problems, because they can discuss the complexity of war and plan a corps-level deployment, often at the same time.

GENERAL LIWEI CHANG stared down at the barren lunar surface from a small viewport in the Chinese Lunar Orbital Station, awaiting Captain Yen Ming's response. Chang knew this man could be trusted. In some ways, he saw a younger version of himself in Ming. So stoic and confident, and ready to sacrifice for the greater good of the people. Ming was the perfect example of Chinese values. The Americans, who were so focused on their own individuality and greed, would not appreciate Ming.

Consumed by social media and focused on their heroic glory days, the Americans had slowly atrophied as a fighting force. The issue, Chang thought, was that they were not able to coordinate. The Americans did not work as one. Free speech and free will were for the individual but served no collective good. The Americans could not understand what it meant for a nation to flow like a river. The river, like China, was a collective society, each water molecule coalescing with others into one powerful force, carving its way through any environment and flowing around any obstacle in its path.

"General Chang?" A voice behind Chang snapped him from his thoughts; turning, he saw the face of Captain Ming on a wall screen. "We are ready to execute on your command," Ming said with absolute confidence.

"Excellent. Execute immediately!" Chang said, cutting the communication and returning to his thoughts.

The general's work—no, his sacrifices—were always for the greater good of his people. He rarely felt personal pride, rarely sought pleasure in personal gain.

However, this time was different. He knew that success in his next task would propel his ascension to the party's inner circle. For the first time in his professional career, his personal satisfaction could benefit both the people and himself.

"What are you two watching?" I say with a groan. The U.S. Space Force habit I am in is small. You optimists would call it cozy. I don't bother looking down from my bunk; they all know I am up now and no doubt feel like playtime is over. I am glad, for once, to be awake. Sleep here is pretty much the only thing to do outside of training and checking equipment. But on the moon, my dreams are always strange. I keep having this recurring dream that I am jumping out of a swimming pool like a dolphin at a waterpark. Before you say I am crazy, apparently it is possible to do that on the moon; I saw it in a Space Force recruiting video, and recruiters never lie!

"Sorry, sir!" chime both specialists Edgar and Carpenter nearly in unison. "We were watching a Pular Mechanics NextTech episode on a new concept for a carbon dioxide to oxygen conversion plant," Edgar states.

"Yeah, just one of them is supposed to reduce the CO_2 emissions for an entire super city!" Carpenter adds helpfully.

"Okay, nerds!" I say, wincing as I slide off the bunk with a thump. "Now that I have been serenaded awake with that quality, super useful information, I think I am officially ready for some training!"

I ignore the collective groan and smile. With one boot on and struggling to put on the other, I yell out, "Will one of you troglodytes please get Master Sergeant Stone?"

Before either of them can get up from their seats, Master Sergeant Stone bounds into the room and shouts, "We have a distress call from the mining camp!"

The room falls completely silent. I am the first to react and shout, "You all heard Stone. Get your equipment on and meet me in the pressure bay in five minutes!" This is our Augmented Assault and Rescue (AAR) team's first call and our primary mission; the only thing we really train for. Well, that and supervising autonomous equipment container drops, but once they are on the ground and establish a connection to the orbital station, they practically run themselves.

With both of my boots finally on, I quickly zip up my Space Force flight suit. In my Space Force "onesie," I hastily grab a nutrient bar (yum) and a water bag and head to the communications room, where Stone is staring at the comms equipment.

I notice right away Stone's blank stare and perplexed look. I say, "Stone, you look like you're the one in distress; what's up?" Stone turns and says, "Sir, it's gone! The distress call was sent out, you can see it right there, but now there's nothing! I have tried to respond but I got no response."

"Okay, no worries. It's not like we have anything better to do today and the trip will make for some great training," I say. I take a moment to concentrate on finishing off the last neutron bomb and throwing it into the trash slot. Did I say neutron bomb? I meant nutrient bar, but for the record, they both contain compressed energy and taste like destructive sadness. So yeah, I call them neutron bombs.

"Go get the guys ready in the pressure bay. I'll be out shortly," I say, nodding to Stone. Without a word, Stone nods back and starts for the door. Trying to lighten the mood, I smile mischievously and say, "Let's go big on this one, full gear and equipment loads. It should be fun! Worst case scenario, it's a comms issue. We get to go for a joy ride on the moon, and Edgar gets a chance to show some new people those sweet tricks our guardian bots can do!"

Picking up the communications handset as Stone leaves, I press the transmit button. "Mining camp, this is Captain Brock Maxwell, responding to your distress signal. Do you read me? Over." I repeat this message several times and even try to radio up to my command, but like Stone, I get no response. With a sigh, I recall the solar flare last week that degraded communications for hours.

Shrugging it off, I figure that as long as we can communicate within our team then we are good to go. Exiting the communications room, I lock the door behind me. Funny, there is no one on the moon for miles; satellites watch this place almost 24/7, and yet we still have protocols to lock up. Before heading to the pressure bay, I scan the crew quarters. I smile, noticing that the two specialists have remembered to shut off the media station for the first time in Space Force history.

U.S. Space Force Augmented Assault and Rescue teams consist of two specialists, a master sergeant, and a captain. Each team member has specialties, but in emergencies, we are all cross-trained to perform the essential functions of the other members of the team. Specialist Carpenter is an expert at maintaining our sophisticated augmented military gear, as well as keeping our lunar buggies (we call them "bugs") and Guardian bots running. Carpenter also makes sure our hab doesn't smell like feet when one of our filters is clogged. Specialist Edgar is our communications and electronic warfare expert. With a degree from MIT, he could have done anything, but he always wanted to go to space, so he enlisted in the Space Force. Foolish as that may sound, the kid is a genius and can bypass any switch on any network. Master Sergeant Stone serves as our senior noncommissioned officer, my advisor, and the team's tactical weapons advisor. He's old, like I think he fought in Afghanistan and Iraq with my father old. Kidding, but seriously, he's definitely older than anyone on the team. As for me, I'm the AAR team leader responsible for this merry band of misfits. AAR team leaders generally have a degree in engineering and graduate from a two-year Special Purpose Operations and Weapons Course, known as SPOWC. Yeah, that name. I definitely get made fun of by other services, but now I can jump higher and run faster on the moon!

For soldiers, precombat inspections serve as a method of assessing the unit's preparedness prior to the execution of the mission. Stepping inside the pressure bay, I begin to put my suit on and scan the area. I see the team finalizing their checks. Carpenter, who has completed his checks on our suits, the Guardians, and the bugs, is halfway into his suit now. Edgar already has his suit on and appears to be dancing to a song no one else can hear while doing data security tests on our Guardian bots. Lastly, I see Stone checking off the last item on his list, completing the check to ensure our suits are functional and fueled. Stone also makes sure we have essential human stuff like oxygen, water, and food. Each member of the AAR team is issued a gauss rifle. It is each of our responsibility to make sure our weapon is functional, and we collectively go through the checks. Gauss rifles utilize a state-of-the-art battery power cartridge that holds metal bullets. Once the trigger is pulled, those bullets are propelled down the barrel faster than fifty meters per second.

Once I put on my suit, I check that the augmentation works. The augmented suit is the heart and soul of the AAR team. It provides a user-friendly augmented reality experience powered by an on-board computer. All of the suits worn by AAR team members are linked through a mesh network, enabling each member to communicate and share data with all other members. As the team leader, I can see each team member's status in the upper left-hand corner of the suit's heads-up display, or HUD. Seeing all status lights are green, I address Stone.

"Stone, are we all ready to go?" I ask while walking toward the door and the button that initiates decompression.

With a smile only concealed by his visor, Stone responds, "All good, sir. We are ready to rock." I think that may be a lunar dad joke and chuckle. Taking one more look around, I get thumbs up from each team member and hit the button. With a hiss, all of the air inside the pressure bay is pulled out, and the door opens.

Outside the hab, each of the team members hops on his own bug. Bugs are designed much like the Apollo lunar buggies with two seats and the motor, battery, and storage in the back. Unlike the Apollo lunar rovers, bugs integrate with the augmentation in our suits and can travel greater distances. For this mission, our bugs are loaded with extra ammo, hab repair kits, extra battery packs, oxygen, water, and of course, "neutron bombs" in case I get hungry for more edible suffering. Taking a moment to update the coordinates of the mining camp in my HUD, I share it with the rest of the team. They will not see what I see. A wide purple roadway painted on the lunar surface by our augmented suit indicates the route to the camp.

Indicating I want to move out, I begin to creep my bug forward, motioning to the rest of the team to follow. Once each team member is on the move, I press a button on my suit to activate team-wide communication. "Team, you all know there was a distress call from the mining camp. As you can see in your HUD, the camp is about five miles away. We take it slow and maintain proper formation. Edgar, I want you by me, making sure those Guardian bots protect our flanks. Carpenter, you take point. Stone, you guard the rear. Keep your heads up and take this seriously."

The trip is short, only taking thirty minutes, as the augmented software inside our suits traces the most efficient route for our bugs. As we are about to crest the last hill, Edgar breaks radio silence. "Sir, Guardian One has eyes on the mining camp... it looks pretty bad. I'm sending the live feed to your HUD now." The live video from Guardian One pops up in the upper right corner of my screen. Taking the whole scene in, I see the collapsed dome of the mining camp, the company logo deflated over its exterior. Small jets of steam appear around the edges, indicating that whatever atmosphere was once inside the camp is quickly venting into space.

Upon arrival, I notice that the door to the mining camp pressure bay has been completely sucked off by the vacuum of space and lies several meters in front of the collapsed dome. Attempting to mask the tension in my voice, I radio Carpenter and say, "Carpenter, I need you to send your Guardian bots to sentry mode, one on each corner of our position." The Guardian bots are just that, bots that serve as our guardians on the battlefield. Circular in shape, Guardians use small thrusters to hover above our position. They are equipped with grenade launchers, automatic gauss rifle, and a vast array of sensors capable of capturing signal and imagery in a wide range of spectrums. They integrate directly with our augmented suits and utilize a limited on-board artificial intelligence when performing certain tasks.

Once Carpenter has the bots moving into position, I sling my rifle and grab ahold of the pressure bay door at my feet, motioning for Stone and Edgar to help me lift it up. Grunting from the effort, I say, "If there is any chance to get some sort of temporary atmosphere inside, we need to do it." Not missing a beat, Carpenter rushes to his bug and grabs a pack of temporary seals and a tool kit. Putting a sealed pressure door onto a hab is never easy, but Carpenter, as his name suggests, crafts a suitable solution with our emergency patch kit, while the rest of the team brings our gear inside.

The main thing to consider when repairing any collapsed hab is equalizing pressure. If someone is on the inside of the next door, the best way to save them is to first create some sort of sealed barrier on our side that can hold air and pressure. To restore the pressure in our now patched and less-than-pristine pressure chamber, our team deploys TAKs, Temporary Atmospheric Kits. TAKs are basically a super pressurized, breathable atmosphere in a can.

Once Carpenter indicates the TAKs have equalized the pressure, I walk up to the door to the living quarters and manually open it. The door slides open easily. A little too easy. I can see right away that for whatever reason, someone inside must have left the door to the living quarters partially open when the pressure bay lost atmosphere.

Looking around the room, I see three bodies lying on the floor, the atmospheric mist from our TAKs swirling around them. Both Edgar and Carpenter look as if they are going to be sick, but Stone stays resolute and focused, saying, "They look like they have been dead for a while." Looking past the bodies, I notice the mining camp command center across the room and motion Edgar over to it. The hab is the standard small hab configuration and as such is almost identical to ours. Scanning the room, I notice something that strikes me as odd. The bathroom door is closed. Normally, in habs, like airplanes on Earth, bathroom doors remain open when not in use. In space, closing the door offers more than just privacy. Closing the bathroom door in a hab temporarily seals the occupant inside, creating a temporary atmosphere that redirects air to special scrubbers, keeping the hab universally fresher. Curious, I walk up to the door and try to open it. To my surprise, it's locked!

"Carpenter, do we have stable atmosphere in here?" I yelled excitedly. "Like, can I take off my helmet right now without dying?" This gets Stone's attention.

Turning his head, Carpenter replies with a hesitant "Yessss," drawing out the s for emphasis. "Sir, please don't do that," Stone admonished. Ignoring Stone, I continue, "I'm not going to take my helmet off, but this door is locked, and I think there is someone inside." Forgetting the two, and possibly my wits, I decided to knock on the door. As both Stone and Carpenter look on with disappointed faces, I place my head against the door and listen. This doesn't help at all; the helmet itself has augmented speakers for an atmospheric assault and adjusts automatically to the ambiance of the room. To my surprise, I hear a knock back. Then another. Both Stone and Carpenter's faces turn from concern for me to concern for the situation. Without warning, the door opens with a whoosh and a woman, in the most raggedy space suit I have ever seen, steps out.

After a few minutes of introduction and explanation, we find that the woman's name is Emily Daniels, a system engineer at the camp. There were only four people assigned to the mining camp. Emily happened to be closest to the bathroom when the pressure bay doors blew. Fearing the hab doors would be next, she grabbed a radio and a space suit and hid in the bathroom.

"Took you guys long enough," Emily says, after slipping into one of our extra suits and sealing the helmet.

"We aren't a pizza delivery service, ma'am," Stone replies, not concealing his frustration that Emily is implying we took our time. Divesting from the conversation quickly, I scan the room again. My eyes land on Edgar, who is plugged into the command terminal, lines of code sailing by faster than I can read. He is in full augmentation mode, the equipment in his suit helping him rapidly digest and understand the data faster than any human alone. Suddenly, the text stops scrolling, and begins to slowly scroll up, then down again. Edgar isn't looking up. Sensing something is wrong, I begin to head toward him. Before I am halfway to him, Edgar yells, "Sir, I don't think this was an accident!"

General Chang wished he could see from his window, but he refused to let his emotions take control of his actions. Gathering himself in an attempt to remove all emotion from his voice, he asked, "You are sure the mining operation is shut down?"

"Yes, General, our team performed exceptionally," responded Ming with a deferential tone.

Through his window, Chang imagined seeing the mining camp's dome collapse, and with it, his work nearly completed. He could have asked Ming for a visual but that would take a few seconds and was not worth his time. He trusted Ming. But trust was not as important as the collective good of the party, or the people. He had to be sure, so he asked, "Are there any loose ends? Did we take care of that Space Force team?"

Ming, always a professional, responded promptly. "My team saw the Americans enter the camp twenty minutes ago. We are setting up an ambush now. All communications have been blocked in the area. We will be ready for you to make an official statement to the Premier in the next hour."

"Excellent. Be sure to notify me when you have closed this account," Chang said, and ended the communication.

Chang had to keep looking forward and let Ming deal with the now. He needed to focus on his message to the Premier, which was really a message to the world. The Chinese lunar expedition had discovered that the U.S. Space Force and mining camp teams were tragically killed in an accident. The Chinese would, of course, publicly investigate the accident. They already had crafted evidence that the American people would believe. After all, controlling information on the moon was easier than on Earth. The Chinese investigation teams would be thorough in their efforts, providing a wealth of information to the U.S. public while carefully denying any contrary information from reaching Earth.

Chang would take his time with the investigation. It was time enough to help the Americans forget about their Helium-3 mining operations on the lunar south pole. It was time enough for the Chinese to take their place. It was time for China, not America, to be the leading supplier of Helium-3. *No*, Chang thought, *it was time for China to be the wealthiest nation in the universe.*

With my heart in my chest, I rush to Edgar's side.

"Who is General Liwei Chang?" Edgar says, not looking up from his work.

"Isn't that the Chinese general in charge of the scientific expeditions here on the moon?" Stone yells from across the room before continuing his debriefing of Emily. Looking at the screen, I see that whatever Edgar has found is highly encrypted. Growing impatient, I ask, "Edgar, what exactly did you find?"

Nodding, Edgar turns around and motions for the rest of the team to come forward. With a few flicks of his wrist, we are all looking at an augmented three-dimensional image of the moon in the center of the room.

Sounding like an obnoxious museum tour guide and pointing at a flashing red arrow on the map, Edgar says, "We are here. About three hours ago, there was a highly encrypted burst transmission sent from here." Another red dot appears on the image of the moon, about a kilometer north of our current position. "Then one single sustained transmission for about thirty seconds at that same location, then nothing." As Edgar finishes, a red circle appears around the red dot indicating the last transmission.

"I ran a trace on the transmissions and they are closely correlated with transmissions coming from the Chinese orbital station."

Before Edgar can continue, Stone cuts him off. "That is hardly an indication of Chinese involvement in what looks to be an accident!"

"I know, I know!" Edgar says excitedly. "But it did get me thinking. Why is the entire command console here encrypted?"

"Wait! It's completely encrypted? Are you sure?" Emily says with a gasp.

"Yes, and it's deleting itself, just like the old ransomware viruses back in the day. Except without the ability to pay to make it go away," Edgar responds. Before we can cut him off again, he continues. "The good news is that I was able to stop it from both encrypting and deleting. Then by transferring the encrypted data to my suit, I was able to decrypt the remaining data. That's the bad news. I found a remote execution command sent to the mining camp to release the seals on both the pressure bay and the hab. It was sent in Mandarin. I was able to translate some information from the Mandarin files, including a message directly to Gen. Chang from a person only identified as 'Ming.'"

"Dr. Ming?" Emily asked, questioning. "He's one of the Chinese scientists here on the moon, conducting research on Helium-3."

Edgar, shaking his head, says, "I don't think he's a scientist,

Emily. There are encrypted maps inside the data that show large deposits of He-3. Problem is that there are Chinese mining facilities placed on top of the facility here. Also, he doesn't write like a scientist. He makes clipped statements like a military officer. No offense, sir! I ran a scan with the speech pattern analysis suite in my suit on all of Ming's communications. The analysis didn't show a match between the scientific documents with his name and the actual message traffic we are seeing here."

No one speaks as Edgar's assessment rings in our ears. I am about ready to step in to break the silence when Edgar's eyes then go wide. Clearly on to something, Edgar asks, "Sir, have you been able to reach anyone from command?"

"Actually, no, I got nothing before we left, figured it was just a solar flare like last week," I say. Which in my defense is fair, I think. AAR teams usually operate for weeks without communications from higher command. We do check in and provide updates as needed. However, most communications to and from the lunar surface are done by automated computer systems that relay information back and forth.

Snapping me out of my thoughts, Edgar says, "Sir, we are being jammed! I was able to triangulate the emissions to here." The same red ring on the image of the moon starts flashing.

"Wait, is that the same location that the Chinese communications came from?" I say, asking the obvious question while picking up my rifle.

"Yes, sir," Edgar says, getting the hint that we are about ready to move.

Walking to the pressure bay, I am joined by Stone. I can tell he can't wait to leave this half-destroyed base. "Stone, I don't have a full picture of what's going on here, but I do know we need to shut down that jammer and relay what Edgar found to command."

With a slightly giddy tone, Stone says, "You got it, sir! We can go on a field trip, but if this goes sideways, you're the one that has to tell Dad!"

Before everyone can get to the pressure bay, my plans (which aren't even plans yet) immediately change when Carpenter comes running over to Stone and me.

"Sir, Guardians One and Two are picking up movement about a kilometer to our north. The Guardian's onboard system has identified four armed personnel in four vehicles, and moving in a tactical formation. Sir, I have confirmed Guardians assessment; these guys are armed and inbound to our location."

"Good work, Carpenter," I say, then turn to Stone. "Tactical formations? That doesn't sound like a scientific expedition."

Gearing up and exiting the mining camp with Emily, we take up positions, with the four Guardians spread out in front of our formation. The Guardians are piloted by Carpenter, who shelters in a nearby crater to our rear with Emily. With Stone, Edgar, and me in defensive positions on the edge of a crater, all there is to do now is wait for the Chinese to arrive.

A grueling minute later, the Chinese can now be visibly seen in tactical formation, heading in our direction. It is clear from our scans that they have not discovered our positions yet. As I flip through sensor feeds and the imagery provided by the Guardians on my HUD, an idea strikes me.

Smiling, I say, "Hey Edgar? Can you hack into Chinese suits?"

His response is immediate; he likely has a similar idea. "Sir, normally, no. However, based on the information left on the hacked mining camp terminal, I have a pretty good idea of how their suits handle message traffic. I think at the very least I can gain access and shut off their communications. Once I gain access to their suits, I will know more about what I can and cannot do," he says, clearly getting excited about the prospect of using his skills against a real threat.

When the Chinese are only three hundred meters away, I aim my gauss rifle in their direction. In my HUD I see a familiar bright blue dot; that's where my gauss gun is aimed at the moment. Next, I start scrolling through a list of fire solutions in my HUD and select the option for "1×2," which stands for one shot, two bullets. A series of red diamonds appear, indicating I now authorize the Guardians to begin tracking enemy targets. While the gauss rifles fire much like a normal rifle, the 1×2 mode allows targets that are fired upon to be simultaneously engaged by the Guardians. Thus, one shot, two bullets. With the targeting solution set, and the Chinese still advancing on our position, I begin to get nervous. I don't think anyone has actually engaged in combat on the moon before. What sort of precedent are we setting if U.S. forces shoot first? What would the fallout be if the Chinese see my actions as an act of war? I know the suits' recordings would show the whole thing, but these days, video proof isn't as ironclad as it used to be. Fake videos are easy to make, and real videos are often difficult to verify. If possible, we need to take the Chinese alive.

"I'm in, sir," I hear Edgar say, pulling back into the present. Seeing an opportunity to potentially deescalate the situation, I ask, "Can I talk to them? I want to let them know we are here and inquire about their intentions."

Without hesitation, Edgar says, "Yes, sir. I have engaged the simultaneous translation software. You will sound like a computer with a British accent speaking Mandarin, but they will be able to understand."

A moment later I see a Chinese flag icon pop up in the top right of my HUD and select it.

"Chinese soldiers, this is Captain Brock Maxwell of the United States Space Force. You are trespassing in a U.S. commercial designation zone, protected by the U.S. government. Please state your intentions clearly. We are armed and will fire if you proceed. Over." All there is for me to do now is wait for a response.

Gen. Chang had never been a patient man. Sure, he pretended to be from time to time. Such is the way of any good Chinese leader. Be patient, but be ready. That was what all of his instructors had explained to him about the Chinese active defense strategy. It was based on waiting for the enemy to present opportunities and the preparedness necessary to exploit them. He was exploiting an opportunity now though, and patience, he figured, could be replaced by violence of action. During the creation of the Chinese lunar security forces, the senior party officials wisely recommended that back doors be placed in all astronauts' spacesuit software. These back doors allowed Chinese commanders to remotely monitor their subordinates' suit cameras and data to ensure that trust was not misplaced and control was absolute. Smiling at the thought of his Party's foresight, Chang pulled up Ming's camera feed.

To his astonishment, he was staring at an American. Tilting his head down slightly, he checked to see if the feed was working correctly. The authentication code matched Capt. Ming's, but clearly this was not Ming. Before he could ponder this troubling turn of events any further, the man began to speak. Well, it wasn't a man; more like a computer with British-accented Mandarin.

"General Chang, this is Captain Brock Maxwell of the United States Space Force. Before we proceed, I want to reassure you that your men are safe. They are currently in the custody of the United States and will be released as soon as they can be safely returned to Earth for trial. We have information concerning your government's involvement in the death of three mining employees for the purposes of taking over their operations here on the lunar south pole. This information, along with the data recovered from the mining camp and your astronauts' suits, has been transferred to the United States government. In the following days, your government will be contacted by the United States Department of State in an effort to negotiate the release of your astronauts. Have a better day. Maxwell out."

I probably should lie to you all and say that we had a massive firefight on the moon and prevailed against the Chinese because of superior American firepower, but as is the case in combat, it is more about luck than anything else. While Edgar hacks the Chinese suits, Carpenter maneuvers the four Guardian bots as close as possible to the Chinese soldiers. Just before the Chinese crest the last hill, Carpenter hides all four Guardians in a lunar crater. This is all Carpenter's work, though I'm sure Stone is guiding him the entire way, like a jockey gently guides a horse around a race track. Once in place, all Carpenter has to do is wait for my command and we will spring the trap. I figure all I have to do is wait until they are close, swarm the Guardians in for a good old fashioned show of force, and they will surrender. I do just that. I give the command and Carpenter goes to work.

The enemy, unfortunately for us, gets a vote. Upon seeing the Guardians surrounding them, the Chinese don't surrender, not even close. What they do is shoot one of the Guardians and fall back into a defensible crater to engage the other three drones. Yeah, that backfired. The good news is that as I rack my brain trying to figure a way to peacefully end this before I lose the remaining three drones, Edgar takes action. Edgar, who now has complete access to the Chinese suits, takes it upon himself to reduce their oxygen and give them all a maximum dose of painkillers, courtesy of the automatic medical care suite in each of their suits. What a mess.

It takes almost three hours to get the four Chinese sleeping beauties back to our hab. We have to make a side trip to the Chinese jammer, where I let Stone use his explosives for the first time on the moon. Boom. Once back at our base, I release a statement to the Chinese and call my command. Why do I do it in that order? I figure it's better to ask for forgiveness than permission. Plus, Carpenter is pretty shaken up at the loss of his drone. I think he even named them. Emily ends up getting picked up by another lunar mission tasked to refit the destroyed mining base. Edgar even helps them upgrade their cybersecurity. As for the Chinese soldiers, it is almost a week until someone comes down from Space Force command to secure them for transportation. I think they are actually happy to be taken by the end of it. Turns out, Ming and his team had enough of our hospitality. That might have something to do with the generous amounts of neutron bombs they ate. Who would have thought they were so universally hated?

Bag of Soldiers

ERIC FOMLEY

Eric Fomley writes speculative short fiction. His stories have appeared in *Galaxy's Edge*, *Daily Science Fiction*, and *Inferno! Volume 6: Tales from the Worlds of Warhammer*. Follow him at ericfomley.com or on Twitter @PrinceGrimdark.

THE BATTLESHIPS in the clouds above me monitor my every move.

I crunch along the sheets of endless ice to reach my fallen brothers. The icy winds of Ghede Prime howl as they blow through the glaciers and try to hold me back.

I see the soldier before I'm standing on the green waypoint in my frosty visor. His body lays at odd angles, his armor shredded from gunfire, face locked in a permanent scream. Blood oozes from his wounds. His head is still intact.

I kneel alongside him and retrieve my drill and microsaw from one of my suit's pockets. Particles of bone and bloody flesh fleck my visor as I drill three holes in a triangle on the frontal lobe of the soldier's skull. I use the microsaw to connect the holes and gently pry the triangle of bone free. Blood and fluid pool and leak from the wound but I can see the silver microchip clamped to the soldier's brain like a spider. I slide the blade of the microsaw underneath and pull the chip free.

I use my free hand to put my tools away and retrieve the cloth bag tied to my belt. I drop the chip into the bag with the others. Organic bodies are cheap to manufacture. The tiny infrastructures that house a human mind, less so. This soldier, and the others I've collected, will live. They'll be given new bodies and sent to the front lines to fight again. As long as the chip is collected, they'll never die.

I stand, look down at the soldier, and think of our plight, our seemingly eternal service to the Dominion. What life did this one leave behind before they took him?

I feel the shock at the base of my brain. It's light, a warning, but it rocks my body with a moment of sharp pain as every nerve in my body prickles simultaneously. The Dominion is waiting. I'm taking too long.

I move toward the last waypoint on my visor. The crystal ice shatters and cracks beneath my boots. The small generator in the back of my environmental suit whines as its power core struggles to keep up with the demanding climate, struggles to keep my organs warm and filter the frigid air through my mask at a breathable temperature. How I wish I could take the suit off and let the elements take me. How long would I enjoy death until I was recovered?

The Dominion fights a war of planets. A tireless fight to own them all. But whatever the strategic or monetary value of this ice rock is, I'll never know. But for them, it's enough to lose lives. The crimson pooling out of my brothers paints color on this colorless world.

The soldier at the last waypoint is dead, his head blown apart, and with it the chip that held his mind. Command must see this through my visor cam because the waypoint clears from my heads up display.

Mission complete.

I pick up my pace as I trudge back to my flyer with the bag of soldiers still in my hand. It will be night soon; the sky is the dark gray of Dominion battleships. At night the hellish conditions on Ghede Prime worsen. My suit would never keep up.

Just before I reach my flyer, I query the onboard AI assistant to fire up the engines and begin the prelaunch checklist. I order it to drop the boarding ramp.

My foot catches the lip where the ramp meets the ground. I sprawl forward and catch myself with my free hand, but several of the chips spill out of the bag and bounce off of the ramp onto the ice.

It's a clumsy move and command rewards my foolishness with a full shock.

I collapse.

I can't keep my teeth clamped as the pain ignites every nerve. Pinpricks like a million knives stabbing every part of my body all at once and I'm alive to feel it. I convulse on the ramp and scream until I think my heart will stop. My skin twitches and spasms when the shock is gone. I can't wipe the spittle from my face or visor until I'm back on the ship and can remove my environment suit. I roll onto my stomach and try to rise as quickly as I can before they decide to give me another. I set about recollecting the chips I dropped.

Except for a few I pretend I don't see.

It's not enough chips to justify them sending another collector. That would be too much of a waste of time and fuel.

I'll be reprimanded, probably shocked again, and maybe more than once. But the unrecovered chips will be shut off. Those soldiers won't be used again, won't ever have to march to their deaths again.

They're free from living like this.

It's all I can wish, as I board my flyer and launch it to meet the battleship up in the clouds, that one day, someone will do the same for me.

ALSO FROM NATHAN W. TORONTO:

Rise of Ahrik
(available now)

Revenge of the Emerald Moon
(available now)

Redemption of the White Planet
(available July 2023)